OTHER NOVELS BY CLARE JAYNE

Campbell & MacPherson Historical Mysteries

Lady Tinbough's Dilemma
The Dead Duke
A Dangerous Past
The Convenient Murder
Mr Guthrie's Double
A Virtuous Man
An Impossible Crime
The Prankster

Dumnonia Mysteries

Murder on Bealtaine Eve
A Fatal Voyage
The Vanishing Thief
Murder By Another Name

Historical Romances

Complications
An Impetuous Romance
Ladies Dancing

CONTENTS

A Dangerous Past (Campbell & MacPherson 3)

Third Book in the Historical Mystery Series

Clare Jayne

1. THE DEATH OF A FRIEND
Edinburgh, March 1789

"MAY I speak to you, miss?"

Ishbel looked up from the medical textbook she had been studying at the sound of a weak, shaky voice that sounded nothing like the usual cheerful tone of her lady's maid. Lucy's face had a pinched, shadowed look to it. Ishbel hurriedly got to her feet and put an arm round her shoulders, leading her to a chair in the bedroom and waiting until she was seated before fetching the chair she had been sitting on at the desk, then placing it opposite that of the other woman. She sat down and asked, "Lucy, what is wrong?"

"I just heard that a friend of mine is dead, miss."

"You have my deepest sympathies. If you need to take some time off from your job to help the family..."

"... I think she was murdered," Lucy interrupted.

Ishbel's heart fell. She had turned her back on the attempts she and Ewan MacPherson had made to solve crimes after the disasters of the first two matters they had been involved with. She might have been able to cope with the result of the Viscount Inderly's court case, where he had received only a fine after causing the death of Aileas Jones, but finding out that Mr Fillinister would hang for killing the Duke of Raden, who had mistreated his sister, had destroyed her faith in the justice of the Scottish law courts. She had rejected Ewan, something she had regretted every day since his departure, because of her belief that they had done more harm than good in their work. The last thing she wished for was to be pulled back into dealing with

1

another murder now.

She could not ignore Lucy's plea for help, though. Lucy had worked for her for nearly five years and had swiftly become a confidante and friend, helping Ishbel in the unladylike pursuits of studying at Edinburgh University and later solving criminal activities while the rest of Edinburgh society showered disapproval down on her. Before Ishbel met Ewan, Lucy had been the only person who was wholeheartedly on her side; even her cousin, Harriette, disliked her academic interests. Ishbel must do whatever she could for Lucy now.

"Tell me everything you know about the crime, starting with how you came to know your friend," she said.

Lucy nodded, agitation fading. She believed that a positive outcome would come from Ishbel being involved in the matter and Ishbel desperately hoped that she would not disappoint her. "Her name is – was Morag Duncan. We grew up on the same street, four houses away from each other and, being the same age, we became good friends and for years we spent all our time in and out of each other's houses, playing together and sharing hopes and secrets. Morag was twelve when she got a job in a clothing factory and family friends let her live with them, as they were closer to where she worked than her parents' house was. She came back to visit them most weeks at first, and I often saw her, but she gradually returned less and less often and, of course, when I was fourteen I came to work for you, Miss, and was given a room here. It must be six years since I last saw Morag but our families still live in the same houses. Ma heard from Mrs Duncan what had happened and, knowing from me about the killers you've stopped, she said you might be able to discover the truth of how Morag died. Will you help us, Miss Campbell? We all need to understand why Morag was killed."

It seemed that Ishbel's desire to escape the world of criminals had failed. She could only resolve to get a better result this time than she had been able to achieve before. "I promise I will do everything in my power to find out what happened to your friend."

2. REUNION

"A LETTER for you, sir."

Ewan took the folded parchment from the silver tray his butler held out. "Thank you, MacCuaig."

The butler withdrew and Ewan broke the thick seal of red wax and opened the letter. He recognised his sister's writing at once and smiled, happy to hear from someone he loved. At least he still mattered to Matilda. It had been three months since he had last seen Miss Campbell, after her assertion that she did not wish to continue her association with him. Even knowing how much he loved her she had dismissed him from her life as if he were no more than a casual acquaintance. Before that he had actually begun to believe that she returned his affection and that they could have a happy life together.

Refusing to allow himself to dwell, yet again, on the past, Ewan took a fortifying sip of chocolate and began to read the letter.

My dearest brother, I have news that I hope will be as delightful for you as it is for me. Lord Picton has grown disillusioned by the growing decadence of London society and has decided to move our family to Edinburgh.

Matilda was coming home. It was what he had always wanted. Seven years older than he, Matilda had been more mother than sister to him for much of their childhood, looking after him while their mother's health declined. Matilda was already gone – living with her husband in London – when their father became ill and the transition from youth to the master of an estate had been a difficult one for Ewan to handle alone. After six years apart, he would have his family back and not just the two of them: Matilda and Picton had three small children, a son and two daughters. Ewan had not even met his youngest niece, born just last year, and could not wait to do so. He returned eagerly to the letter, to find out what else his sister had to say.

I told Lord Picton that you would have no objection to us residing with you while he finds a house for us and I hope this will cause you no inconvenience.

On the contrary, Ewan would have wanted nothing else. He stood, letter still in his hand, and walked across the room to ring the bell. His butler appeared at once.

"MacCuaig, would you have the staff make the necessary arrangements for us to receive visitors for an extended stay? My sister and her family are returning here."

The butler's craggy face brightened into a smile, one of only a handful Ewan had ever seen. "To live, sir?"

"Yes."

"On behalf of all the staff, may I express my pleasure at the news?"

"Thank you, MacCuaig. It has considerably brightened my own day."

"When should I tell the maids to have the bed chambers ready, sir?"

Ewan looked down at the letter, his eyes searching through it for a date and he smiled again when he found it. "They will be here in a fortnight."

"And we shall be ready to receive them, sir."

When his butler had left, Ewan resumed his place at the dining table, his meal forgotten as he read the remainder of the letter.

Rebecca and Jamie are excited to see their Uncle Ewan again and I know you will adore Anne, who is the most lovely and well-behaved baby. My husband and I have only one concern, that I am certain you can resolve for us. We have heard reports from acquaintances in Edinburgh that you have become entangled with a woman of sordid background and have been spending time in the company of people of low birth and character. I am certain, knowing as I do your upstanding character, that a misunderstanding must have occurred and wait for you to allay our fears. Your loving sister, Matilda.

A chill ran through him as he read the final sentences and he felt offended on Miss Campbell's behalf at hearing that she had been described in such a way. He had not mentioned his recent involvement in criminal matters in his latest letters to his sister as he

4

had anticipated explaining them to her in person in his intended summer visit to her family in London. He had been sure she would understand his motives in undertaking the work if he could see her face-to-face and tell her how important it was to the families involved. He should have realised that she would have kept in touch with some of her friends, who would have given her the worst interpretation of his actions.

He stood up, intending to go to his study and compose a letter to Matilda that said why he had begun solving crimes with Miss Campbell, but then he realised with a stab of pain that there was no longer any urgent necessity for him to do so. His relationship with Ishbel was over, as was the work they had undertaken together to catch criminals. All he needed to tell his sister was that he would explain the matter to her fully when he saw her and that it was in the past and could, therefore, cast no stain upon the character of their family.

Picton was the old-fashioned type – rather stuffy in Ewan's private opinion – so, although it was the last thing he wanted, perhaps it was for the best that his time spent hunting down murderers was over.

The door to the dining room opened and MacCuaig told him in a tone that dripped with disapproval, "Miss Campbell is here to see you, sir."

Ewan's heart jumped at the words. It was almost as if she had responded to his thoughts about her. Ishbel would not call here at his home except for the most important of reasons. Could she have changed her mind and decided to marry him after all? He could think of nothing else that would bring her here after they had been out of touch for so long. "Please show her in."

"If that is your desire, sir." MacCuaig did not quite give a sigh of displeasure but it was a close thing. He vanished, reappearing an instant later with Ishbel, who had a young woman with her that Ewan recognised as her lady's maid. At least she was not here without a chaperone, although he doubted that Edinburgh society would view her visit to an unmarried man's house as anything other than scandalous if anyone discovered it. Such behaviour would, of course, be forgiven if an engagement announcement swiftly followed it.

"Miss Campbell." He bowed to her.

She responded with a curtsy that, as always, was a touch clumsy. It was still endearing to him. "Mr MacPherson."

She was as beautiful as ever, outfitted in a green walking dress and paisley shawl that complemented her pale complexion and the rich copper-coloured curls that showed beneath her favourite wide-brimmed hat. Her expressive eyes held a nervous expression that he at once felt the need to alleviate.

"Please would you have a seat? May I have refreshments brought in?" While it was still breakfast time for him, he knew that she would have been awake for several hours, her attendance at university lectures meaning that she did not keep to the fashionable hours of late nights and a breakfast at ten or eleven in the morning.

"No. Thank you." She sat down on an oak chair near the fireplace, the firelight giving warmth to her delicate features. "I know I should not have called upon you here but I could not request that you visit my home after our last meeting. I have no right to ask such a thing but a friend of Lucy's –" She gestured to her maid " – has been killed and I have agreed to help discover what happened."

He struggled to take in the words. She was not here because she had missed him or had regretted turning down his offer of marriage. Anger arose in him at the callousness of her behaviour in coming here for nothing more than a piqued interest in a criminal matter. "You wish for my assistance?"

"Yes, I..."

"... I fear I cannot help you," he said stiffly. His sister loved him and he would devote himself to her family instead of longing for a lady who had made clear more than once that she did not care for him. "I have more important concerns that need attending to."

"Of course." She dropped her gaze to her gloved hands and, despite everything, he immediately wished he had not spoken so curtly. She continued, "I apologise. It was wrong of me to speak to you over something like this."

She got to her feet and he did the same. "Good day, Mr MacPherson. I am truly sorry that..." Their eyes met once more and hers were agitated, full of turmoil he wanted to understand. "I apologise."

She hurried from the room, her maid behind her, before he could decide what to say to her and he was once more left alone.

3. THE SEARCH BEGINS

HOW STUPID she had been to turn to Ewan after the way she had left things between them. She should have expected no other response when, after such a long absence, she spoke only of a crime. There was so much she had wanted to express of a far more personal nature but, with Ewan's butler and Lucy in the room with them, she had not been able to do so and now she had hurt him all over again. She might never have another chance to tell him how wrong she had been and how much she had missed him.

"What should we do, Miss Campbell?" Lucy asked, recalling Ishbel to the present and the fact that she was standing on a doorstep in the rain. She had made a promise to Lucy and she would keep it even if it meant working alone. She already suffered the censure of high society; she could hardly make her social standing much worse.

"Do you think your friend's parents would be willing to talk to me about Morag or, after such a recent loss, is it too soon?"

Lucy's worried frown vanished and she gave a smile. "I'm sure it'll bring them relief to know that you're looking into what happened."

Ishbel instructed the coach driver to take them to the address Lucy gave and forced herself to concentrate on the murder and put thoughts of Ewan to one side for now.

The street where Lucy and Morag grew up had the look of one of the poorer parts of the city with cobbled grey pavements filled with refuse and a long line of thin houses joined together that rose high above them as if trying to blot out all sunlight. The area could not be more different from the one where Lord and Lady Huntly's residence resided. There were no trees or carriages other than their own nor finely dressed people strolling about at a leisurely pace. Instead, grubby children played in the road, the stench of horse manure and household refuse filled the air and underfed people hurried along, glancing towards Ishbel – a wealthy outsider – with curiosity or nervousness.

Lucy led the way to a house that was identical to its drab neighbours and rang the doorbell. A mousy-haired woman answered it and stared at Lucy, before embracing her, tears in the woman's eyes as she drew back. "I'm glad to see you, lassie. It's as if the last few years never happened to have you here again and I wish to God that they hadna."

"I'm really sorry about Morag, Mrs Duncan. I woulda done anything to stop harm coming to her if I'd known."

Mrs Duncan patted Lucy's cheek. "I know, lassie."

Lucy gestured to Ishbel. "This is Miss Campbell, the lady Ma told you about. She wants to help discover who killed Morag."

Mrs Duncan made a deep curtsy to Ishbel. "Bless you, miss. No one else cares about my girl so I prayed you'd be willing to find the truth for us."

"I will, Mrs Duncan."

"Please come into the parlour."

She took them through a damp-smelling corridor to a cold dark room with an unlit fire and, after asking Ishbel and Lucy to sit down in the wooden unadorned chairs, she lit a candle which she placed on the table between their chairs. At once a soft glow made the shadows around them come to life, revealing a dining table on the far side of the room on which lay Morag's dead body, with glinting copper coins over her closed eyes, a superstition that was meant to keep her spirit from wandering. The coins made it look as if her eyes were moving in her grey face. It was usual for a corpse to be laid out in such a way and Ishbel was used to the sight of dead bodies from her medical studies, although she was acutely aware that this was someone dear to the living people in the room.

Lucy went pale at the sight of her dead friend and Ishbel took her hand and squeezed it, before turning to concentrate on their hostess. The woman was thin to the point of looking emaciated, skin pulled tight over protruding cheekbones and jaw, and the black mourning dress hung loosely on her.

"Mrs Duncan," Ishbel said, "the last thing I want is to distress you but do you think you could tell me what you know of Morag's death?"

"Of course, miss. A member of the Town Guards came to the door yesterday and told me Morag had been found dead in an alley in Miller Street, to the west of the city. The man said it was probably some cutthroat wanting to rob her but Morag never had any money and she had no reason to be there."

"Was it near her job? Lucy mentioned that she worked in a clothing factory."

Mrs Duncan swallowed and looked away in an uncomfortable manner. "No. She stayed at the factory for a couple of years but someone accused her of stealing and she was fired. She had a few different jobs after that but she dinna have anything lately."

There was something ominous in Mrs Duncan's reaction to the question and Ishbel began to fear that Morag might have been involved in something illegal. "Was she still living with family friends at that time?"

"No, she wasna." Mrs Duncan hesitated and rubbed at a fraying patch on the chair, the tears in her eyes overflowing and running down her cheeks. "She had a room somewhere. She dinna tell me where it was."

Lucy comforted the woman and Ishbel did not ask any more questions, not wanting to make Mrs Duncan more upset. It was clear that Morag had had secrets, perhaps dangerous ones, and Ishbel had the disturbing sensation of once again beginning an investigation the answers to which might bring misery instead of relief to the family involved.

4. DOUBTS

"MACCUAIG, WOULD you have my carriage readied for immediate departure?" Ewan said as he left the dining room and headed for the stairs.

"Yes, sir."

He ran up the staircase to his bed chamber where Rabbie, who had been sitting polishing a pair of boots, legs sprawled in front of him in a relaxed pose, got abruptly to his feet. "Are you leaving already for the club, sir?"

"No." He had forgotten that he had arranged to meet McDonald and Chiverton for luncheon. "I will have to get one of the footmen to let them know I cannot join them today. I have an urgent errand."

Ewan donned his jacket, which made him realise he had not been wearing it when Miss Campbell visited. He doubted it would change her opinion of him either for good or ill, but he heartily disliked the thought that she had seen him in a half-dressed state. He belatedly noticed that Rabbie had been holding out a hat and gloves to him for some time and took them.

"When will you be returning, sir?"

"I am not sure. I need to see Miss Campbell."

Rabbie gave a nod that had a hint of satisfaction to it. "Yes, sir."

"It is not what you think. She called on me about a murder, not for any personal reason."

"If she had something difficult to deal with and wanted your help, that sounds personal to me."

As he walked out of the room and left his home, Ewan wished he felt so certain. In truth, he was still hurt and offended by all that had passed between them and he wanted to stay away from her. He was not the least bit certain that he could trust her not to break his heart again and, with his sister wanting him to lead a conventional life, he should stay out of the latest crime. He thought of Matilda's letter and of the possibility that she and her husband might change their minds about moving to Edinburgh if they believed Ewan was involved in something scandalous that would affect their reputations. It was enough to give him pause, torn by his heart in two directions, but searching for a killer was not something his conscience would allow him to let Ishbel pursue alone. The thought of her getting into a dangerous situation without him there to help her was insupportable. The fact that she had chosen to take up the matter and force him into such a painful decision, after everything else she had done to him, was infuriating, though. He wondered how she had been persuaded to look into such crimes again when she had been so adamant before that she was finished with the work, and then he recalled her saying that the corpse had been a friend of her maid. Perhaps she had wanted this no more than he did.

His carriage was waiting outside and he told the driver where to go, the address a familiar one to the man by now. As the horses got moving he tried to decide what he would now tell his sister. His decisions had not affected his family while they were living in London, but if they were all living here that would change. On the other hand, he was doing nothing illegal or immoral; on the contrary, he was trying to help people who had no one else to turn to. Matilda had always been a caring person, so surely she would understand? It was not her he had to convince, though. Her husband was the one who would say yay or nay to moving here and, from what Ewan knew of him, Picton was a born politician, who cared more for appearances than the truth.

Ewan had found no good solution to the problem when the carriage halted outside the familiar elegant residence. He paused – this was his last chance to change his mind – but with Ishbel pursuing something risky, there had never really been a choice.

His tiger, an eager-to-please boy, held the carriage door open for him and Ewan descended and approached the house. Ewan used the door knocker to rap on the front door and the family butler immediately opened it.

"I am here to see Miss Campbell," he said, although he was certain the man would have already guessed that much from his many previous visits.

There was a hesitation and then the butler asked him to wait and vanished into the drawing room. Ewan frowned, wondering what was going on. After a moment the butler returned and led Ewan into the room, which quickly explained the initial hesitation: Ishbel was not there.

"I fear that my cousin is not home." Lady Huntly's tone was unusually polite, which made him wonder uneasily what Ishbel had said about him. "Did she expect you? If she is at the university she could be gone all day."

He had no idea where Ishbel was but it was certainly not the university. It sounded as if Lady Huntly was unaware of the new investigation, which put Ewan in an awkward position. He did not want to reveal something that would bring Lady Huntly's ire down on Miss Campbell but he also knew that Lady Huntly was too astute to be fooled for long by evasions. "I was given to understand that Miss Campbell wished to speak to me but a time was not mentioned."

"That is unusually thoughtless of her." Lady Huntly frowned. "Will you wait or call again later?"

That was the pertinent question. Frustration tempted him to say that he would leave and not return, but it was not actually Ishbel's fault that he had changed his mind. He would just have to engage Lady Huntly in safe conversations about social activities and acquaintances. "Unless it is inconvenient, I think I should remain here. It might be important."

"Very well."

They sat down and waited.

5. HOW MORAG DIED

"THIS IS where the dead girl's body was, miss," the guard told Ishbel and Lucy.

Ishbel had thought that she might have to resort to asking Jed, the caddie, to find the guard who had been called out to remove Morag's body, but they had found him themselves immediately after asking someone at the Tolbooth Gaol where the officers worked. He was a broad, grey-haired man who, like many of his companions, wore the red uniform of a Highlands soldier and he looked down at the two women with clear disapproval when Ishbel explained that she was looking into the death.

He had agreed to bring them here, though, and Ishbel studied her surroundings. The streets at either end of the winding alley were in the centre of the city and teemed with people, but the alley itself was stained and foul-smelling and, therefore, mostly deserted. Ishbel assumed that was why Morag had been killed here.

"How was she murdered?" she asked.

"Her throat was slit," the guard said shortly.

Lucy made a distressed sound and Ishbel put an arm around her while noting the discolouration on the ground that could be blood. The light rain of the last few days would have washed away some of it and spread the marks around but, standing here, it was easy to imagine how the events had happened.

The guard looked at them and said, "Perhaps it would be best to leave such violent matters for men to deal with, miss."

What men? He and his group, already known for their lack-lustre work, would not pursue this death further and, if she did not look into it, who would? "My friend is distraught because she was friends with Morag Duncan. That is why we wish to find out who killed her."

"I'm sorry you've had a loss," he said in a gentler tone, "but it's obvious what happened. She was killed by some vagabond looking for coins."

"Her mother said that she would have had no money."

"She was mistaken. There was a guinea under the lassie's body that must have been missed when she was robbed and, around this part of the city, cutthroats will murder someone without a second thought for even the hint of money."

A guinea was a lot of money for a young woman without a job to have on her, another suggestion that Morag had been up to something illegal. "What time of day was this?"

"The body was found early afternoon and wouldna have been there for long."

Ishbel looked up and down the alley. The far entrance was not visible from here but the other was, the sounds of horse hooves and the calls of street sellers clearly audible. "Why would she not have cried out for help if she was being attacked?"

"The killer would have murdered her first and then robbed her. I expect it was over before she even knew someone was behind her."

Ishbel thought about this, picturing herself in Morag's place, and then asked, "Who reported the murder to you?"

"A merchant with a milliner's shop over there." He pointed in a northern direction.

"Do you know his name?" She did not have any paper or quill with her to write down the information but she could remember it.

"I know his shop."

"Would you show it to me?" He hesitated and she added, "Please. The young woman's family just want to know what happened."

"Aye, all right." He walked ahead of them and they followed.

"Did he or anyone else see the murder?"

"No. He said that a child found the body and told him about it." He stopped walking and gestured to a small shop with a bony finger. "That's the one."

"Thank you. We appreciate your help." She was not sure whether or not to offer him a coin for his assistance, not wanting to offend him since he was here as part of his job. She paused too long and he touched his cocked hat to her and strode away. Ishbel turned to Lucy, who still seemed shaken by finding out what had been done to her friend. "Would you prefer to wait in the carriage while I ask the merchant what he knows?"

"No, miss. I'm well."

They walked into the shop. A couple of women – working class but with enough money to dress smartly – were admiring hats. The seller, who had been trying to tempt one of them to try on a ribbon-covered bonnet, glanced round and, at the sight of Ishbel, left the women and hurried over.

He had striking grey eyes that looked almost white in the light from the window and wore a plain brown outfit. He bowed to Ishbel and said in an English accent, "Welcome, my lady. As you can see, I have a fine stock of hats and ribbons for you to choose from."

"I am not here to make a purchase." She explained who she was and their purpose in coming here and saw his expression fall at the realisation that he was not about to gain a wealthy client.

"I'm afraid I can't tell you much. A local boy ran through the alley as a shortcut, on an errand for his mother, who sells flowers on the street further up. He said he nearly fell over the body. The sight of her scared him and, not sure what to do, he came in here. I went and took a look and saw that the poor girl was definitely dead, so I did my duty and reported it."

"Was there any sign of anyone who could have been the killer?"

"No, Miss Campbell, happily for me." He pulled a face at the idea of such an encounter. "This must have been a while after she was killed as the blood had run everywhere. It was a mess."

"Did it seem to you like the result of a robbery?"

"I couldn't say, miss. I know nothing of the criminals around here – I wouldn't have anything to do with them." He sounded offended.

"No. Of course. Thank you for answering my questions." She looked about and gestured to the least extravagant of the hats in sight. "I would like to purchase that."

He perked up as took down her address, so he could send the bill for payment.

Lucy took the hat box to carry it for her and they left the shop and returned to the carriage, where the driver was waiting – making conversation with a couple of the women selling food on the street – to take them home. There was a look of strain on Lucy's features as the footman helped them into the carriage and Ishbel resolved not to bring her along when asking further questions, as hearing the full details of Morag's death must be painful for someone who had been her friend. She should have thought of that before.

As the horses got the carriage moving, Ishbel said, "I will keep looking into this but it seems likely that the town guard was right about Morag being killed for money."

"I wonder where the money came from," Lucy said, echoing Ishbel's thoughts. "Perhaps she had a new job that she hadna told her family about yet."

"Maybe. I will find out."

"Thank you for your help with this, miss. At least I can tell Morag's parents that she died quickly. She canna have felt much pain if she dinna have time to call out, can she?"

"No. I think it would have been over before she knew what was happening."

"Poor Morag. She never had a chance to make much of a life for herself."

Ishbel pictured the woman, younger than herself, a living, vibrant version of the unearthly figure laid out in her family's home, with mousy hair like her mother's. She could almost believe that she could feel Morag's spirit watching her progress and, even as she shivered, she harshly dismissed such a superstitious idea. The carriage came to a halt before Ishbel could think of a reply for her maid. There was another carriage in front of the house and, even through the mist of rain, Ishbel recognised it at once.

Ewan was here.

6. TRUCE

LUCY TOOK the hat box upstairs along with the gloves, hat and caraco jacket Ishbel had been wearing, leaving Ishbel free to go and speak to Ewan.

She had never before felt so nervous about seeing him. His anger at her for approaching him about another murder had been palpable and she did not know what to say to change his attitude. She had treated him badly and she could not take it back. He was here, though. That suggested that he had, for some unknown reason, decided to make peace with her.

She glanced in the hall mirror with its frame of gold leaves and attempted to smooth down her damp, windswept curls then, knowing it was unfair to keep him waiting any longer, she straightened and walked into the drawing room.

Ewan was there sitting in a chair near the flickering orange glow of the fire, Harriette opposite him. The fact that they both held teacups and that there were empty plates on the mahogany coffee table nearby suggested that Ewan had been here for a while.

He stood up to bow to her and, while she curtsied in response, Harriette, still relaxed on the chaise longue, said, "Finally! Isobel, you and I must have a long discussion later about good etiquette. It is hardly polite to invite someone to call on you and then vanish for hours at a time."

Since she had not asked him to do so, the words made her falter, confused, before she realised Ewan had been protecting her by avoiding saying that she had come to his house. She had not been thinking but that had been a highly misguided thing to do. "Yes. That was extremely rude. I apologise, Mr MacPherson."

His gaze was a touch wry. "I imagine you did not expect me so soon."

"No." She had not dared hope that she would ever see him again.

"I imagine Mr MacPherson wishes to know why he was summoned here," Harriette prompted, clearly too curious about what was going on to leave them alone. Social convention would say that she must always be present while an unmarried man was visiting Ishbel, but Harriette had given up trying to chaperone them long ago. Ishbel suspected that her cousin liked Ewan, although that did not cause her to spare him her sharp tongue and sarcasm. No one escaped them.

She spoke as if to Ewan but, since he knew the basic facts already, they were aimed more at letting Harriette know what was going on. "My maid, Lucy, informed me today that her childhood friend, Morag, was killed. I have agreed to find out what happened and hoped to enlist Mr MacPherson's assistance."

"Not again!" Harriette glared at her. "Have we not had enough of murders and other equally disreputable subjects?"

"Lucy needed to know how her friend died. I could not refuse her."

"And no doubt you will be equally unwilling to refuse the next person who asks." Harriette picked up her fan and got to her feet, the layers of her long skirts swirling around her. "Since murder is not a topic I find in any way agreeable, you may continue your discussion without me."

She left the room and Ishbel turned to face Ewan, her mouth suddenly dry. "I am so sorry I was not here and that I approached you for such a reason as this. I had wanted to speak to you many times – I should never have turned you away after the last murder. Can you forgive me?"

"I do not know." The quietly spoken words sent a chill through her. "I am not happy to be here. It puts me in a more difficult position than you realise. However, it would not be gentlemanly of me to allow you to get into a potentially dangerous situation alone, so perhaps you should tell me what you know about the murder."

This was not how she wished to leave the conversation about their relationship, but his words made it clear that he had no interest in anything else she might say about it. He had never used this cool tone with her before and she could only hope his attitude would change in time. They sat down and she told him everything she and Lucy had discovered so far about Morag's death. "There might be little left to find out," she concluded, "but I would like to know where she got the money that she had on her. The guinea left behind is not a small sum for a working-class woman. Her mother's reactions also made me think that Morag could have been involved in something dishonest."

"Then it is possible that robbery was not the motivation for her death. A thief would usually be more thorough than to leave a guinea behind, I should have thought, unless he feared that he was about to be discovered."

"The streets at either end of the alley are busy, so he might have believed someone would see him. The merchant who saw the body said that there was a lot of blood..." She paused, considering it. "I think it likely that the killer would have got blood on his hands and probably his clothing. He could not have gone far without being noticed."

"Then he either lived somewhere nearby or was not afraid of being seen."

"A habitual criminal with a dangerous reputation?"

"Exactly," he said. "Jed Cassell might be able to tell us if there is a known thief who has killed in that way before."

"Surely such a person would have been hanged?"

"Only if he was caught. What people know and what a barrister can prove are two different things."

"Yes, that is true." She had found out in the court case against Viscount Inderly that the truth could be manipulated, when his barrister had done his best to ruin Ishbel's reputation to convince the jury her evidence could not be relied upon. She dismissed the sting of how he had treated her and remembered something else she had wanted to mention. "Also, the merchant thought that the crime had been committed some while before the body was discovered because of the amount of blood on the ground. From a medical point-of-view that is not necessarily true: if someone's throat was slit open there would immediately be a great deal of blood. The murder might have only taken place minutes before Morag's corpse was found, or it could have been a lot longer. The body was laid out at her parents' home but she has been dead too long now for me to be able to give a better idea of exactly when she died."

"Then it happened some time in the morning or middle of the day yesterday?" he checked.

"That is right."

"It might sound cruel to disturb the family's grief again but you said you only spoke to Morag's mother and that there were things she seemed to be hiding. I think we need to talk to both parents and ask them to tell us all they know before we can proceed any further."

It was the parents who most wanted answers about Morag's death so she did not think they would mind answering more questions. "If her father has a job with regular hours, he is likely to be at home in a few hours."

"Shall I call here so that we can go to the house together at that time?"

"Yes, please do."

He left her and, despite the murder and the unresolved problems between them, she felt a thrill of pleasure to be working on a new criminal enquiry with Ewan.

7. A FATHER'S ANGER

"IT WAS only a matter of time before something like this happened," Mr Duncan said, a dark look in his eyes as he shot a glance at the body lying on the table a few feet away. He was a large man with broad shoulders and a restlessness to his movements. "She mixed with all the worst kinds of people."

"She was friends with my lady's maid, Lucy," Ishbel pointed out, offended at the idea that he could be speaking about her in this way.

"Lucy is a good girl, the sort of daughter parents can be proud of. She hadna seen Morag in years and dinna know what she'd turned into."

"Fergus!" his wife objected, tears in her eyes.

"She had money on her – a lot of money – when she died. You know what that means?" His tone to his wife was savage.

"We do not know what it means," Ewan said quietly.

"It means she stole it!" Mr Duncan shouted. "It means that her last act on this earth was cheap and illegal."

He pushed past Ewan and left the room, the front door slamming a moment later.

Mrs Duncan wiped the tears from her face. "He's grief-stricken, that's all. He canna show it any other way."

"We never meant to cause you more grief in telling you about the guinea," Ishbel said.

"You havena, miss. I dinna believe she stole again after promising us she wouldna. She canna have. Something else was going on."

"Perhaps we should sit down?" Ishbel suggested and put a hand under Mrs Duncan's arm, helping her to a chair, which she did not so much sit in as collapse into.

"I'll make a pot of tea," Connor, Morag's brother, said. He had kept out of the argument and his face remained shuttered, his thoughts unreadable. He had been introduced when they arrived and described as working with his father as a sawyer, although he could not be more than thirteen years old. He had the same dark hair as his father but otherwise took after his mother, with the same blue eyes and thin face.

He vanished from the room and Ewan and Ishbel took seats facing Mrs Duncan, who looked over at her daughter's corpse as she said to them, "I ken what you must think of her after hearing that, but Morag had a good heart. She stole money that first time from another worker on impulse."

"This was when she lost her factory job?" Ishbel checked. She had clearly already heard something about this, although it was new information to Ewan.

"Yes, miss. It was awful for her the way she was treated and it embarrassed our family. She was nearly taken to trial over it and realised she might have been transported or had a hand chopped off as punishment. It terrified her and she swore an oath to us that she'd never do anything like it again. We dinna see her every day so she could have had a new job, couldn't she?"

She appealed to Ishbel, who nodded. "Yes, she could."

Connor appeared with a wooden tray containing a tea pot, jug of milk and cups, a couple of them chipped. The water must already have been heating over the fire for it to be hot so quickly. Mrs Duncan immediately got up and poured each of them a cup, Connor taking his and sitting on the wooden floor beside his mother's chair. He was either wary or shy of the two strangers in his house.

Ewan took a polite sip of his tea, which tasted a bit sour, as if the milk used was going bad. He asked, "When had you last seen Morag?"

"Three days ago, sir," Mrs Duncan said. "She came round on the Sunday evening, as she always did."

"Did she seem preoccupied – upset – about anything?"

Mrs Duncan hesitated. "No, sir."

"She asked about her father," Connor said, then flushed when all eyes turned on him.

Mrs Duncan said his name in a warning tone and then explained reluctantly, "I was married once before and my husband died. Mr

Duncan dinna like it being spoke about."

"What did Morag want to know?" Ishbel asked in a careful tone.

"Just the usual: what was he like; how did he look."

"Did she say what made her ask about him now?" Ewan asked.

"She dinna have to, sir. It was her birthday a week ago and that often makes her think about him. I dinna know why – Mr Duncan loved her as much as he loves Connor. He was her real father."

"Could she have asked for another reason?" Ishbel asked. "Could a member of her father's family have got in touch with her?"

"No," Mrs Duncan said quickly. "That's impossible."

"Did she talk of anything else when she saw you?" Ewan checked.

"I canna think. She asked how we all were and helped me with the cooking. What else?" She looked at Connor.

"She said she was trying to find work," Connor said, "but she always says that."

"She meant it this time, I'm sure," Mrs Duncan said firmly. "Perhaps she wanted to surprise us and only tell us about the job once she'd started it or maybe she hadna got it yet."

"That is very possible," Ishbel said, although Ewan could see that she was just trying to ease Mrs Duncan's mind.

"Mr Duncan said that Morag mixed with the wrong people," he said. "Do you know the names of any of them?"

"There were several women – lassies her own age – she spent time with." Mrs Duncan told them their names and Ishbel wrote them down, using the parchment, quill and bottle of ink she had brought with her.

When she had finished writing, Ishbel glanced at him and he interpreted the look and said, "We should leave you now."

"You'll let us know what you discover?" Mrs Duncan asked with a look that was part hope and part dread, as they got to their feet.

"Yes, of course," Ishbel said.

Ewan looked over at the dead body of Morag, neatly laid on the dining table. She had been dressed in white and he could see the gash across her neck. It occurred to him that it must have taken someone – probably her mother – a long time to wash all the blood off her body and hair. An act of love by a grieving parent and he knew then that, whatever they found out, it would not help this family.

8. FIRST IDEAS

"I CANNOT see that her real father is relevant," Ewan said the next morning, sitting in the library of Ishbel's home. It felt odd to be back here in the room that had become so familiar, as if the estrangement between Miss Campbell and him had never occurred. It had, though, and he could not afford to let himself forget it.

"He might be," Ishbel disagreed. "She was thinking of him a few days before her death and her mother's reactions were, once again, guarded. If he had been a criminal and Morag had asked about him to the wrong person, it could have been dangerous."

"Perhaps. But who could she have asked? Mrs Duncan said he had no other family."

"She said it was impossible that anyone could have contacted Morag, which is not the same thing."

"Well, Morag certainly does not seem to have told her family much about her life, which means we need to speak to one of her current friends or acquaintances in order to learn more about her. It might also be useful to visit the factory she was fired from and get the full details of the theft."

"Lucy will probably know which factory it was," Ishbel said. "We could go there now to discover more about her early problems."

"Certainly," he agreed. "While you ask your maid, is your cousin at home? There is something I wanted to ask her."

Ishbel looked at him with interest in her dark eyes. In the past she would have asked him what he wanted to know but now, probably because of the uncertainty of their current relationship, she held her curiosity in check. "I believe you will find her in the drawing room."

They stood up and, with a touch of awkwardness, headed in different directions. He did indeed find Lady Huntly in the drawing room and, unusually, her husband was with her. After they had all exchanged greetings and Ewan had asked about Lord Huntly's job, he got to the subject he had wanted to bring up. "My sister is returning to Edinburgh with her husband and three children. I wondered, since you know everyone in the ton, if you had heard of anyone who has a house to rent? There is no urgency, as they will want to look over anywhere for themselves, but I thought it might assist them to know what is available."

"Would I have met your sister?" Lady Huntly asked.

"You might have. Matilda is seven years older than me so she was out in society earlier, although she married Lord Picton and left Edinburgh for London six years ago."

"Lord and Lady Picton," she said with satisfaction. "Yes, I recall them both. They will likely want a good-sized establishment in the new part of the city." She tapped her fan on her hand, silent for a while, and Lord Huntly returned to his book. "Lord Ashton and Mr Daniel MacRay both have houses that might be suitable. Are you acquainted with them?"

"I am not."

"I will ask them to have their cards delivered to you."

"I am much obliged to you, my lady."

She waved this comment away with her fan. "I imagine it will be pleasant for you to have your family nearby."

He smiled. "That is true. Matilda and I were always extremely fond of each other."

"How nice."

He could tell she was getting bored of the conversation now and so he got to his feet and took his leave of them, still thinking of Matilda as he left the room. He could see her now, a young girl with long dark ringlets, reading him stories and racing about with him across their country estate. They had both grown more sombre after their mother's death, Matilda taking over the running of the house, busy with adult responsibilities but always finding time to spend with her little brother. He knew it would never be like that again but he hoped they could regain the affectionate relationship they had always shared and that he could be a good uncle to her children as they grew up.

Nearby voices penetrated his thoughts and he saw Ishbel walking down the curving staircase, her maid beside her. He smiled at them and Lucy said, "Thank you for agreeing to help with this, sir. It means a lot to me. It's just such a shock having someone you know die suddenly and not having any idea how it came about."

"I fear we may discover things about your friend that you might not like," he said.

"I know Morag wasn't perfect," Lucy said. "She always had dreams of being wealthy and, for someone of our class, that's the kind of ideas that can lead to trouble. I just want to know what happened. I dinna keep in touch with her and perhaps I coulda helped her if I had, so I feel as if I owe that much to her."

9. JED FINDS OUT MORE

JED CASSELL whistled softly to himself as he strode away from Mr MacPherson's house and back towards the High Street. It had been a few months since he had last worked for him and he enjoyed the work Miss Campbell and Mr MacPherson gave him. They always paid generously for his time too.

He reached the busy street and saw several of his colleagues, visible at once in their blue aprons, standing at the Cross, waiting for someone to hire them.

His friend, Billy, looked round as Jed approached and grinned. "Where've you been then?"

"Mr MacPherson wanted me to ask around for a new murder he's enquiring about for the family. The dead woman is Morag Duncan?" He made the last sentence into a question to see who knew the name and Lachlan Brown, the oldest man there at around five and twenty years, gave a knowledgeable nod.

"Oh, aye," he said. "The lass who was murdered in the alley a few streets away."

"That's her. Do you know anything about Morag?"

"I've heard her name somewhere," Lachlan said, scratching on his beard.

"Caddie!" called out a smart-looking gentleman from the window of his carriage.

"My turn," Billy said and ran over to find out what errand the man had for him.

They watched him go and then Jed turned back towards the

group. "There's good money in it for anyone who can help me find out anything useful: who the lassie's friends were; if she had any enemies or was caught up in anything illegal; what she was doing when she was killed; that kind of thing."

"Aye, I'll ask around," Lachlan said and the others agreed.

Jed left them waiting for hire and headed to the alley where Morag Duncan had died. It was good to be back out in the streets where he felt at home, having spent yesterday forced by the Town Council to have a day of schooling. They took it seriously that the men they employed should be intelligent, strong and of good character, since they might be entrusted with money or expensive goods or be needed to show initiative. As a result, caddies had a good reputation, better than the Town Guards they sometimes worked for.

Jed paused to take in the blood stain on the ground. Someone had scrubbed at it but the cobblestones still had a slight red glaze. The woman had apparently been only slightly older than him and it made him think that Death was a companion to everyone, waiting to claim each person. He gave a shiver and hurried out to the shops in the street where the alleyway began.

Everyone nearby had heard of the murder, so it only took one question to have the milliners shop pointed out to him, whose owner had seen the body and alerted the Town Guards. The man was middle-aged, with grey eyes, light brown hair and an accent Jed – who was knowledgeable about such things – recognised as being from the north of England.

"Had you ever seen the woman before?" Jed asked, after the man had told him about finding the body.

"To be frank with you, I don't know," Mr Carter said. "There was so much blood that it was obvious from five or six feet away that the woman was dead, so I never looked properly at her. Miss Campbell told me her name, though, and I didn't know it, although some of the other shopkeepers said they'd spoken to her."

He told Jed their names but, before Jed could leave, Mr Carter said, "We don't often have murders in this part of the city, particularly something that brutal, and it's got people worried. Some of the people – particularly some of the women who work along here – would likely pay for you and some of your colleagues to light the way to their homes. Most of them probably couldn't pay much, though."

"I'd be glad to do it," Jed told him, "and I'll mention it to the other caddies."

He bowed to Mr Carter and walked out, heading for a nearby jeweller's shop. The owner – a small, portly gentleman – said, "Aye, I met the dead woman. She came in here about four months ago looking to sell a necklace and two rings. She told me they'd been gifts but I dinna believe she'd come by them honestly, so I sent her away."

"Have you seen her since then?"

"No."

Another shopkeeper had a similar story but no one nearby had seen the woman on the day she died or, at least, without knowing what she looked like, none of the street sellers were aware of having seen her. The young lad who had first found her could give no more information than Mr Carter had: he'd been running an errand for his ma, had seen the body covered in blood and had run to tell the nearest person he knew about it. No, he hadn't known her, although he'd had nightmares about her death since then.

Lachlan caught up with him several hours later with some extra information and agreed to help him provide protection while walking sellers to their homes.

Jed would ask about some more before letting Mr MacPherson and Miss Campbell know what he'd found out so far. His own guess would be that Morag Duncan had not been as honest as she should have been. Whether or not that had got her killed, he didn't know.

10. REPERCUSSIONS OF THE THEFT

"MORAG DUNCAN – aye, I remember her," said Mr McLain, the manager of the linen factory where the dead girl had worked. He spoke loudly to be heard over the noise and bustle around him, the large building full of men, women and children who were weaving flax, using looms and carrying bolts of material about. "A pretty girl but too outspoken. I'm not shocked to hear that she got herself killed, although I woulda thought it would be a hanging."

"She was only twelve when she came here," Ishbel said, disliking the way he dismissed Morag's death.

"Many of our workers start at that age or younger. We expect their parents to have made sure they understand right and wrong. Morag was always chattering away, bothering the other workers."

"Did she admit to the theft?" Mr MacPherson asked.

"Aye. She dinna have a choice as the money was found in her pocket. She took half the wage of an older woman, Mrs Black, and thought sobbing over it and saying how sorry she was would be enough to save her."

Ishbel imagined the terrified child Morag would have been. "What happened?"

"I fired her on the spot and turned the matter over to the law."

"And after that?" Mr MacPherson said.

"No idea. I never saw her again."

"Could we speak to the woman she stole from?"

"She's not here. Mrs Black left to raise a family a while ago."

"Do you remember anything more about what happened?" Ishbel

asked.

Mr McLain began to his head and then paused. "Wait now. It was Old Angus of the Town Guards who took her away. He's still with them, although he must be five score years by now. Ask him."

"Thank you, we will," Mr MacPherson said and they returned to his carriage.

The Town Guards had their own homes but they reported to the Tollbooth Gaol in the heart of the city and an officer there told them how to find Old Angus – who was not to be confused with Young Angus or Gussie, who also worked there. Old Angus had his own carpentry business, which surprised Ishbel, but Mr MacPherson told her that most of the Town Guards had other jobs as well as that.

"Morag Duncan was little more than a bairn when she took that money," Old Angus told them, as he sat in his workshop, a half-made travelling chest in front of him. He was white-haired but his gaze was sharp and there was clearly nothing wrong with his memory. "Between her tears and her mother's tears, it was never going to go court. Lord Tain isna a harsh man and he sorted it out to everyone's satisfaction."

"Lord Tain? The solicitor?" Mr MacPherson asked.

Ishbel had heard his name mentioned by Harriette but had not met him.

"Aye, that's right," Old Angus confirmed.

"Did you get the impression that Morag's remorse was genuine?" Mr MacPherson asked.

"Aye, I did. She came from a decent family – I could tell from their reaction that they were shocked by what she'd done. I woulda hoped she could put that behind her and make a good life for herself after that, so I'm sorry to hear that she's dead."

They thanked him and left, the sound of hammer against wood following them into the street.

"Should we see if Lord Tain knows anything of Morag's life after the theft?" Ishbel said. "He might have checked up on how she was behaving after that."

"Certainly."

They drove to the law courts and found the offices where Lord Tain and his assistants worked. Lord Tain had streaks of silver in his hair but was still attractive and possessed of an air of vitality. His clothes were of the highest quality, but his strong local accent suggested that his peerage had been gained through his work, rather than being hereditary.

He gave Ewan a searching look. "It's, er, Mr MacPherson?"

"You have an excellent memory, sir," Ewan said and introduced Ishbel to him.

Lord Tain smiled at them both in a genial manner and gestured for them to sit. As they all did so, he asked, "Does one of you have a legal problem?"

"No," Mr MacPherson said. "We actually have some experience of solving crimes. We are looking into the death of a young woman who was a client of yours some years ago. Her name was Morag Duncan."

"Yes, I recall the case." His brow creased. "She's dead?"

"She was killed in what looks like a robbery, but her family asked us to find out more about it. We wondered if she was still involved in crimes or if she really had put such things behind her after this," Mr MacPherson explained.

"Aye, I see."

When he said nothing more, Ishbel prompted, "Old Angus of the Town Guards told us that the case never went to trial."

"No." He paused again, presumably trying to recollect the details from so long ago. "Morag was a child and the money was returned to its owner, who was happy not to take the matter any further."

"Did you ever hear that she might be involved in other crimes?"

"No. I honestly believed that the theft was a piece of childhood folly she hadna understood the consequences of. I hate to think that my leniency might have led her to think she could get away with more illegal activities."

"We do not know at this point that she had done anything else," Mr MacPherson said since Lord Tain was looking regretful over the situation. "Her family did not know of any such thing and her death might well have been what it looked like: a violent robbery."

"Would you let me know the outcome of your enquiry?"

"Yes, of course," Mr MacPherson said.

It was only when they got outside that Ishbel looked around and recognised where they were.

"Morag was killed in one of the alleys near here," she told Ewan. She had entered it from the street below and could not judge, from this direction, which one it was. "I believe it was either there or there." She pointed to an alley behind the law courts and another one street over from them.

"That is an odd coincidence. I suppose it is a place criminals would be forced to visit but I wonder what brought Morag near here."

"Perhaps her friends can tell us," Ishbel said.

11. MORAG'S PAST

AS LUCY helped Ishbel change into a more elegant afternoon dress to attend a select tea party at Mr Chiverton's new home, she told her maid what she and Mr MacPherson had discovered so far.

"Everyone we spoke to believed that Morag would learn from her mistake and commit no further crimes, but we do not yet know if that was true."

"I never even knew she'd lost her job at the factory," Lucy said as she stood behind Ishbel, who was seated at dressing table, arranging her hair. "She must have been too embarrassed to talk about it. I was nervous when I came here and I was older than Morag and you were always kind to me; I've heard the noise and seen the mass of people that work in those factories and Morag was too young, at just twelve years. It wasna fair sending her there at that age. I'm not excusing what she did..."

"... I understand," Ishbel said at once, "and I agree completely. The factory manager seemed like a callous man too – it is terrible to think of young children working long hours in such difficult surroundings."

"She had an adventurous spirit," Lucy recalled with a smile as she teased curls into place. "She longed to see London and Paris and would create in her head the elaborate dresses she would wear. There was no harm in it: she just wanted more in her life than drudgery. If she coulda learnt to be a seamstress or something like that, working with pretty clothes, she woulda been happy but she never had the chance."

"Did she ever mention her father to you?"

"Mrs Duncan's first husband? Aye, she wished she coulda known him. I think she liked to imagine him as some fine gentleman, although she knew that wasna true. She got along well enough with Mr Duncan, but they were different kinds of people and he never understood her need to dream."

"Did she ever mention anyone connected with her father that she might have tried to contact?"

Lucy paused, a comb motionless in her hand, as she thought about it and then she resumed her occupation. "I think the lack of all other family and Mrs Duncan's unwillingness to talk about him made Morag think there was some mystery surrounding him. I doubt it was true, though. I expect his death was a painful subject for Mrs Duncan and I know Mr Duncan had a jealous side – I dinna think he wanted to be reminded that Mrs Duncan had ever been close to another man."

"Did the family ever mention the name of Morag's father?"

"Not that I heard. Why are you interested in him?"

"It was just that her brother said she mentioned him during her last visit to her family, but it was probably nothing."

Lucy finished arranging Ishbel's hair in long fluffy curls, pinned over one shoulder. "There," she said with satisfaction. "That looks just right."

Ishbel smiled in the mirror at her before turning and standing up. Lucy fetched a warm shawl and her hat and gloves.

As Ishbel put them on, Lucy said, "I haven't put you in a difficult situation with this business, have I, miss? I was thinking only about Morag when I asked you to help and now you've had to go to Mr MacPherson for help and look into another crime. Had you wanted to stop enquiring into such things?"

"It was not so much a decision as a feeling that the work Mr MacPherson and I had done had not helped anyone. The court cases freed the Viscount Inderly, a cruel man who caused a young woman's death, and Mr Fillinister is likely to be hanged for protecting his sister."

"It seems to me, miss, that you shouldna take responsibility for actions that aren't yours. Everyone knows what kind of man the viscount is thanks to what you found out and Mr Fillinister chose to kill a man. It isna your fault that he has to pay the price for what he did."

Enough time had gone by that Ishbel could see the wisdom in these words. Perhaps she had judged both her own and Mr

MacPherson's actions too harshly. "I had never realised that I would miss looking into crimes."

"With Mr MacPherson?"

"Yes," she admitted with a smile. "I missed him the most. I was saddened over the results of the last two crimes but I never should have ended my acquaintanceship with Ewan. I thought at the time that I was not good enough for him, but he never once seemed to think so."

"I should think not," Lucy said in an indignant tone. "He would be fortunate to be married to you and he knows it."

Ishbel smiled at these words, but the expression quickly faded. "I do not know if he can ever forgive me for sending him away."

"If you love him, miss, you have to find a way to convince him to."

12. MISS CHIVERTON TAKES AN INTEREST IN MURDER

MISS FIONA Chiverton kept a smile locked in place as she stood in her brother's new house and greeted his guests. It was an unconventional mix of people, half aristocrats and half actors, but everyone seemed in good humour. All except her.

She saw Miss Campbell arrive and her mood brightened. They curtsied to each other and she said, "I am so glad to have someone here I can talk with about interesting subjects."

"Are the rest of the guests so dull?" Miss Campbell asked with a smile.

"The subjects discussed so far have been horses and plays. Not that I have any objection to either of those, but I would much rather hear about the exciting people you meet at the university and during your enquiries about criminals."

"Mr MacPherson and I have, in fact, begun looking into a new matter."

"What is this?" Mr McDonald said, approaching them, a glass of wine in one hand. "You and MacPherson are not mixing with lowlifes again?"

Fiona contained a sigh with difficulty. She had no idea why her brother, Eddie, would do all in his power to stay away from their brother, Henry, on the grounds that he was insufferably stuffy, and then choose to be friends with someone equally tedious. "Miss Campbell and Mr MacPherson do not mix with criminals," she corrected him. "They catch them."

Eddie overheard some of their conversation and pulled Mr

MacPherson with him to join them, Alex following. "So what scandals are you dealing with now?" he asked.

"A young woman was murdered in what looks like a robbery," Miss Campbell said.

"It seems as if there may be some mysteries to uncover, though," Mr MacPherson added. He smiled at Miss Campbell but Fiona noticed that the look never reached his eyes. A few months ago Fiona had been certain that an engagement would be announced between them and the idea had made her glad, if a touch wistful. When she was younger she had harboured some romantic feelings for Mr MacPherson – what young girl would not like a man who was so kind, handsome and good-natured? He had never treated her with anything except impersonal politeness, though, and she had learned how differently a man in love behaved after her coming-out ball, when a number of men had tried to court her in a flatteringly ardent manner. And, when she had met Miss Campbell and seen her and Mr MacPherson together, it had been obvious how well suited they were, but then the crime enquiries had stopped and Mr MacPherson had inexplicably taken to spending more time with Eddie and his other friends.

"If anyone can discover the truth, it is the two of you," Eddie said to them.

Another smile passed between the subjects of the conversation, but there was definite discomfort too. Fiona wondered what could have happened. Had one of them met someone else? If so, then why were they working together again now?

"I thought you had decided to give up such dealings," Mr McDonald said, an edge to his voice.

"They apparently do not want to give us up," Mr MacPherson said and Eddie laughed.

"One cannot escape one's fate," Alex said in a deliberately theatrical tone.

"Just so," Mr MacPherson agreed and Miss Campbell shot him an unreadable glance.

"So who is this relative of yours who left you this inheritance?" Mr McDonald asked Eddie in an unsubtle change of subject that was thoroughly exasperating to Fiona, who wanted to hear more from Miss Campbell and Mr MacPherson about their work.

"My maternal grandfather was generous enough to leave me a

considerable sum in his Will," Eddie explained. "It has allowed me to leave my parents' house..."

"... Escape," Fiona said with feeling, "and heartlessly leave me behind."

"That is not a very ladylike way to speak of your family," McDonald said, sounding as judgemental as her father and older brother and, since it was none of his business, she glared at him.

"I would gladly have brought you here to share this house," Eddie said, which she could not entirely believe, since it would have made it far less convenient for him and Alex to spend time together, "but our parents would never agree."

So now she was stuck at home, under her family's control, and she no longer had Eddie there to make it bearable. She was tempted to marry the next person who asked her so as to get away, but she was sadly too pragmatic to do any such thing.

"Are you at least enjoying being more involved in society's entertainments?" Miss Campbell asked, referring to the fact that now Fiona's coming out ball had been held, she was invited to more events.

"It is enjoyable in the way that a cream cake or a new dress is pleasing. They are all rather superficial."

Eddie put an arm round her waist. "Miss Campbell, have you been turning my sister into an intellectual?"

"I can take no credit for her own good sense," she responded.

As she enjoyed the complement, Fiona caught Mr McDonald's disgruntled expression. No doubt he would find himself a placid, conventional wife one day who loved nothing more than to attend balls and dinner parties. She shuddered inwardly at the thought.

"You should attend more plays," Alex said, smiling fondly at her. "Shakespeare is an expert at opening the mind to new philosophical ideas."

"I would enjoy that," she said.

"But nothing vulgar," Mr McDonald interjected, once again attempting to spoil everyone's good mood.

Fiona turned away from him to face Miss Campbell. "Do tell us more about the new crime you are looking into."

13. ILLEGAL ACTIVITIES

"MORAG IS dead?" The young woman paled and Mr MacPherson quickly took her arm and helped her to a chair, which she sank into. Following the list of names Mrs Duncan had given them, she and Mr MacPherson were at the home of Betsy Dale, a working-class woman of around twenty whose cheeks and lips were stained with rouge.

"I fear so," Ishbel answered as she got out parchment, ink and a quill to write down anything useful that was said here. "I am sorry. We assumed that you would have already heard about it."

"No. I only saw her a week ago. What happened to Morag? When?"

"She was killed several days ago in what looks like a robbery and her family asked us to find out what happened."

"But you're aristocrats," Miss Dale said, looking at their clothes with puzzlement and a touch of envy. Her own gown was brightly coloured and cut low at the chest, with no lace wrapped above to make it more modest.

"We have solved similar crimes. My lady's maid, Lucy, was good friends with Morag when they were younger and asked me to help."

"Aye, Morag mentioned Lucy," Miss Dale said.

"Do you know if Morag was involved in anything that could have become dangerous to her?" Ishbel asked as Mr MacPherson took a seat on the chair beside hers, in the stark family parlour. His behaviour to her was more relaxed today, after the interlude at Mr Chiverton's abode.

Miss Dale hesitated before answering the question. "I dinna ken anything like that."

"How did you come to know her?"

There was a slight relaxing in Miss Dale's posture, as if the last question had worried her and this one did not. "I first saw her looking into the shop of a modiste, trying to get a glimpse of the dresses. Morag could obviously never afford to have clothes made in such a place, so she interested me. I walked over and we got talking about clothes and then about our ambitions. She was fun and smart, so I knew she'd get along well with the people I mix with. She was looking for somewhere to live, where her family wouldna be constantly checking what she was doing, and I had another friend with a spare room, so I introduced them."

"What is this friend's name?"

There was another pause but Miss Dale answered this time. "Nan Smith."

The name was one of the ones Morag's mother had given them. "So Morag stayed there with Miss Smith?"

"Aye, with Nan and George, Nan's brother."

Shock rippled through Ishbel. No wonder Morag had refused to give the address of her lodgings to her parents.

"There was nothing improper going on," Miss Dale continued, seeing her reaction. "Nan and George needed the extra money from the rent and Morag needed a home with people her own age. It suited them all."

"How could Miss Duncan have paid rent?" Mr MacPherson enquired. "I understood that she was not employed at that time."

Miss Dale laced and unlaced her pale hands. "I dinna ken."

"Miss Dale," Ishbel said, leaning towards her, "we have no interest in causing harm to anyone. We are here solely to find out how Morag died and you can rely on us to be discreet over anything in her past that was not entirely legal. We already know about the money she stole when she was working in a cloth factory."

"George got her doing the odd job for him, but you canna tell him I told you."

"We will not," Ishbel promised.

"She wasna stealing or anything like that. She just took certain items to where she was told to and everyone made a bit of money from it. It wasna exactly illegal."

If Ishbel understood the young woman correctly, Morag had sold stolen items to the kinds of people who did not care where those articles were obtained, which was extremely illegal. Mr Duncan had been right in saying that Morag had mixed with the wrong people, ones who had got her heavily involved in the criminal world.

"I wouldna have introduced Morag to them if I thought it would get her into any trouble," Miss Dale went on. "I just wanted to help her."

The fact that she meant this was written across her features.

"I hope you will never get involved in such activities," Ishbel said and saw Miss Dale give a guilty start, "because they are very likely what led to her death."

14. A PERSONAL CONVERSATION

NAN AND George Smith proved far more circumspect about their criminal endeavours than Betsy Dale had been. Their home was a flat within a four-storey house that had rats running along the corridors. Given the slovenly state of the rooms, with food and clothes on the surfaces and floors, it was not surprising that rodents were drawn to the building. Nan Smith had the same gaudy style of dress as Miss Dale, but was far more forward in manner, making eyes at Ewan and brushing against him as she showed them the room Morag had rented from them.

"How did Morag pay you for the room?" Miss Campbell asked in an innocent tone. "We understood that she had not had a job for some time."

"We dinna ask her private business," George Smith said from behind them. He was a tall, lanky man with suspicious eyes in a handsome face. If he had switched on a more charming manner, Ewan suspected that Smith would not have had any difficulty in persuading Morag back into criminal behaviour, probably convincing her, as he had clearly done with Betsy Dale, that there was nothing really illegal in the jobs he got the young women to do for him.

"We weren't greedy," Nan added, sitting down on the windowsill and looking up at him in what was probably meant to be a winsome manner, that had no effect on him. "We liked Morag and if she couldna always pay us, we dinna worry."

"How kind of you," Miss Campbell said with a fair imitation of sincerity. "You must have spent a lot of time with Morag, so was she in any trouble that you knew about?"

Nan Smith looked at her brother, who answered, "She'd been a bit moody for the last week, as if something was on her mind, but she dinna tell us what it was."

"We were really upset to hear that she was dead, weren't we?" Miss Smith said and her brother made a sound of agreement. Neither of them looked particularly grief-stricken. "We were told it was a robbery. Morag was a good-natured lass – she wouldna have done anything that would make anyone want her dead."

"No, that's right," Smith agreed. The two of them were far more careful of what they said than Betsy Dale had been and so they asked no more questions, Ewan glad to remove Miss Campbell from such a disreputable place.

Having had dry weather when they entered the building, a deluge of rain was now pouring from the slate grey sky as they left. Ewan's driver jumped down from the carriage and held the near-side door open as soon as he saw them, holding out a gloved hand to help Miss Campbell climb up. She hurried to take it and, once she was seated, the driver closed the door and hastened round to open the far-door for Ewan, who also wasted no time in getting into the dry interior.

"Where to next, sir?" his driver checked.

"To Miss Campbell's house," Ewan said and the driver nodded and closed the door, giving the two of them privacy. Ewan attempted to brush some of the excess water off his jacket but did little more than smear it about.

The horses got moving, pulling the carriage smoothly along, and Miss Campbell said, "Do you think we should believe what Mr Smith said about Morag being concerned about something before her death, or is it more likely that he was just trying to divert us from the fact that he and his sister had got Morag mixed up in criminal work?"

"It was difficult to tell," Ewan said, trying to ignore the dampness seeping through his clothes. "I feel some sympathy for Morag, though. She had no chance of keeping her behaviour honest after meeting those two and it was always going to cause her misfortune."

"I agree." Miss Campbell's expression was pensive.

"Perhaps we should tell Morag's parents and your maid that she had been involved with dangerous people and leave the matter there. I fear that anything more we discover will just distress them."

He was not surprised when Miss Campbell shook her head. He knew her well enough by now to understand that her conscience would not permit her to leave such a matter only half resolved. "No. We have found out nothing about her actual death and, given what we have learned, it is possible that we might be able to uncover the identity of her killer. It no longer seems likely that she was just murdered in a robbery attempt." She looked across at him. "Unless you do not wish to be further involved in this?"

The idea clearly bothered her, so he said, "I am content to see this matter through to its conclusion."

"Thank you. Mr MacPherson... If you do not wish to discuss this, I will respect your decision, but I would like to try to explain why I previously ended our association."

He had regretted not giving her a chance to speak on the subject before as he very much wanted to understand why she had acted as she had. "I would be glad to hear you."

"You know that my family's past is not without stain and that my own behaviour is viewed harshly by the ton."

"I never cared about that," he said, wondering how she could think otherwise after knowing him all this time.

"I know." She gave a nervous smile. "You have always been extremely considerate and understanding. However, I feared that you might one day regret your association with me and that you might come to wish that you had a wife who would increase your social standing, rather than lessening it." Before he could deny this, she continued, "While we worked together and I felt that we were helping others, I could tell myself that our relationship was a positive one. I reacted badly to the results of the last two crimes we looked into, feeling at the time that our actions had caused suffering to innocent people. It made me feel that I was harming your life too and, irrational as that decision was, I honestly believed that your life would be better without me in it." Having expressed what she needed to, Ishbel let out a shaky breath and awaited his reaction.

She deserved equal honesty so he paused to collect his thoughts before replying. "When I met you, I had decided that I wished to marry. There was something lacking in my life that I thought I could fill with a wife and children. I was wrong. I needed to feel I was doing something useful with my life and not just living a frivolous existence. I have found that by looking into crimes – no matter that the outcomes have not always been what we hoped, it has been work that I could be proud of, that challenged my abilities and knowledge. If such endeavours negatively affect the way society sees me, I do not care. If my association with you harms my standing in the ton, I will never object. This is a life that I choose, regardless of your own decision in the matter. My feelings for you are something separate." He was still unsure of her feelings for him so he resisted the desire to express his love and ask her to marry him again. He could not bear another rejection that would damage what relationship they currently had. "I would ask that you banish thoughts of society's opinions of you and your family from your mind and know that they have no effect on me."

"Then we are..." She hesitated. "... friends?"

"I sincerely hope so." And perhaps, in time, she would want a closer relationship with him.

15. JED SHARES HIS FINDINGS

MR MACPHERSON came into her house to discuss Morag's death further and they discovered Jed Cassell, the caddie, standing dripping in the hallway.

"Please join us in the library, Mr Cassell," she said and ordered refreshments be brought to them and the fire be built up.

The butler gave an unhappy glance at Mr Cassell, who still wore his stained work apron, but simply replied to her request, "Yes, Miss Campbell," and left to make the arrangements.

Ishbel led the way into the library, glad that the caddie was here with them. The personal conversation with Ewan had been an emotional one and she was uncertain as to how she felt about its outcome. She was relieved that he seemed to have been willing to forgive her for the unintentionally cruel way she had treated him, but she was not sure if he still wished to marry her and that hurt. As was her want, she reacted to emotional turbulence by finding something else to focus her mind on.

A housemaid followed them in and got the fire blazing, then unobtrusively retreated.

There were two chairs already arranged in proximity to the fireplace, so she waved Mr MacPherson towards one and took the other, saying, "Mr Cassell, will you bring a chair over so that we may all dry off?"

He obeyed at once, his youthful features pinched with cold. It was midway through March and, as Ishbel felt the heat of the flames begin to thaw her own body, she thought that she would be heartily glad when this long, freezing winter was finally over.

"Do you have news about Morag Duncan's death?" she asked him. They had given him the details of the murder a couple of days ago and knew his job, and that of his fellow caddies, travelling the streets of Edinburgh each day to run errands for a small fee, would allow him to find out far more details about people than they could. His help during their previous enquiries had proved invaluable and, in some ways, she thought of him as part of their small team.

Jed Cassell gave a distracted glance at the butler and footman who had entered the room with the refreshments she had asked for, before answering in his familiar Highlands accent, the tone more lilting than the local Scottish accent. "Aye. When I asked around, I was told that Morag was the go-between, passing stolen items off to criminals."

"What manner of criminals?" she asked as she poured out three cups of tea and handed two of them to the gentlemen. Mr Cassell gingerly accepted the delicate china, holding it in both of his large hands.

"It sounds as if Morag was known to some rough people."

"What are their names and where can we find them?" Ishbel offered round the plate of scones and then opened her reticule to get out her parchment, ink and quill.

Mr Cassell answered her question and she wrote down the information as he added, "If you have any questions for them, it'd be best if I asked them for you, Miss Campbell. They aren't the sort of people either of you should come in contact with."

This was the kind of comment Harriette would make, so Ishbel was tempted to dismiss it, until she recalled that both Mr MacPherson and Mr Cassell had been struck during the investigation into the Duke of Raden's murder, when they had spoken to the wrong people. The incident that caused Mr MacPherson's sore, swollen eye and Mr Cassell's bleeding nose was definitely something she did not want a repetition of. They would need to be more careful this time. "I also had a thought last night that the guinea coin found beneath her corpse might be important. We always felt that it was a lot of money for her to have with her."

"From what we have since discovered, it was probably the payment for stolen items," Mr MacPherson said, his face half in shadows cast by the dancing flames.

"But that would not be a reason for her to be killed, unless a robber did see her with the money, but then why would he leave the coin behind?" she said. "No, Morag knew about a lot of illegal behaviour – what if she decided to blackmail the wrong person and the guinea was her payment?"

"It would certainly be a good reason for someone to harm her," Mr MacPherson agreed, although he did not look convinced.

She had no evidence for her theory, but everyone they had spoken to so far had seemed to like Morag. If she did not die for any personal reason then it must have been something to do with the work she undertook for George Smith.

"Did anyone mention the name George Smith to you?" she asked Mr Cassell, who was still holding his cup of tea as if it might attack him and had put his plate on his lap so he had his other hand free to take a bite out of his scone.

He hastily swallowed, his Adam's apple bobbing, and said, "Aye, Miss Campbell. The lassie was thought to be acting under his orders in handling the stolen things."

"Did anyone say anything more about what manner of person he was?"

"No, but I can find that out."

"That would be useful," she said, "and we would be glad to know if he was involved in any other kinds of criminal work."

She hoped that the answers he found out would tell them a great deal more about the danger Morag had got into.

16. A RELUCTANCE TO TALK

"I SHOULD call alone on the people Jed told us about," Mr MacPherson said when Mr Cassell had left them.

"No," Ishbel immediately disagreed. "A criminal is more likely to see you as a threat and attack. That was what happened before over nothing more than a misunderstanding. If we approach the first shop together and show an interest in making a purchase, it will make our visit look innocent."

"And how will questions about a murdered woman be made to seem innocent?"

"We could tell a half-truth," she suggested, finishing her cup of tea. "We might say that my lady's maid knew Morag and, having heard the shop mentioned by her, we wished to see it?"

"We might avoid suspicion that way."

"Shall we leave now?" She glanced at the window, where rain was hurling itself at the glass. It was disheartening to go out again when her clothes had only just got dry, but her studies at the university had got her used to ignoring the elements.

"If you wish."

If her dash from the front door to the carriage was less than ladylike, she did not care. As Mr MacPherson took the longer route around the back of the carriage to join her, Ishbel felt sympathy for the driver and young boy acting as tiger who would remain on the outside of the coach in the rain during the journey.

It only occurred to her when she and Mr MacPherson were standing inside the first shop on her list, that it might not be convincing to suggest to the owner that they were strolling round Edinburgh High Street in such weather with no hidden purpose. Added to this was the fact that there were no other customers in the shop and that it was not the kind of fashionable place that members of good society would visit. They could not take back their actions now, though, since the proprietor was approaching them. He was a plump, middle-aged man with a jaundiced complexion who wore a style of clothes that had gone out of fashion some years ago.

"Welcome to my establishment, sir and madam. May I show you any particular ornament or furniture?"

"My wife and I are decorating our first home," Mr MacPherson said, startling her. She told herself this was the obvious excuse for them to be here together, but her heart continued to beat more quickly as he went on, "My wife had heard that we might find some pleasing knick-knacks here."

"May I ask who recommended my humble shop to you?"

This question gave Ishbel the perfect chance to use the explanation they had made up. "My lady's maid had heard it mentioned by a friend, Miss Morag Duncan. I imagine she must regularly visit your shop."

"I'm afraid I dinna know the name, but please allow me to show you some of my wares."

Ishbel took careful note of the items around her, although had they come from the home of someone she knew – which was unlikely – she would still be unlikely to recognise them. They did not manage to escape for some time and Mr MacPherson carried a newly purchased lamp that he would probably not dare display given the likelihood that it had been obtained by dubious means. Their journey to a second, similar, shop produced the same denial by the owner of any knowledge of Morag Duncan. After this lack of success, there seemed little point in continuing.

The lies did tell them something, though. The shop owners were known to have regularly bought from Morag so, if they refused to admit to knowing her, it was confirmed that these dealings must be illegal.

Mr MacPherson returned Ishbel to her house, the rain obligingly ceasing now that they were going indoors. He agreed to meet her again the next day, after a lecture she wished to attend, and they would see if they could make better progress.

17. BRIBERY AND THREATS

"I LIKE it very much," Chiverton said, looking around the spacious drawing room. He wore blue jacket and breeches and his blond hair was tied back beneath his tricorne hat.

"As do I," McDonald agreed. He looked similarly smart, although his attitude was less alert than usual.

"You made the same comments about the last two houses we inspected," Ewan pointed out as he studied the elaborately carved furniture.

"You can hardly expect incisive remarks at just passed nine in the morning, my friend," Chiverton said and yawned to prove his point. "It is practically still the middle of the night."

"I am grateful to you both for accompanying me. My sister and her family will arrive in little over a week and I do not feel in any way prepared for it."

"What is wrong?" Chiverton asked at once, seeing that this was not actually about houses.

"Some acquaintance of my sister's told her about my work with Miss Campbell and Matilda disapproves. I have not had a response from her to the letter I sent trying to put the matter in a more favourable light."

"Then perhaps you should think of your family and cease involving yourself in crimes," McDonald said, the cutting words spoken in a concerned tone that he could not take offence at.

"Your life is your own," Chiverton disagreed at once. "No one but you should have a say in what you do."

"Nonsense," McDonald said, turning towards him. "Everyone has responsibilities to those they care about. You simply get away with more because you are a younger son."

"Did you happen to notice that, aside from Fiona, none of my family attended the tea party I held at my new home? My father and brother are barely speaking to me, nor allowing my mother and Fiona to do so, because someone may see Alex spending time at the house and speculate. I chose to put my feelings for Alex ahead of their plans for me. I believe I had a right to make that choice, but it did not come without a heavy sacrifice." Chiverton looked from McDonald to Ewan. "This is your decision but you must decide what you are willing to lose for it."

Nervous, Ewan said, "I have made up my mind that this – catching criminals – is how I intend to spend my life. If I lose my standing in society and gain the reprobation of my sister's family I will accept that. This path interests me more than any other. It is what I want."

Chiverton stepped forward to pat Ewan's shoulder. "You may rely on continuing to have my friendship."

They both turned towards McDonald, who huffed out a breath. "I think that the two of you are foolish and reckless, but that is not new. You will not lose my goodwill either. I suppose you still wish to marry Miss Campbell too?"

Ewan nodded. Having a closer relationship with Ishbel meant even more to him than the crime work. "I do. If she will have me. In truth, I am not sure what she wants from our relationship."

"When did you last propose marriage to her?" McDonald asked.

"I asked her some months ago."

"Only once?" McDonald checked.

"Well, yes."

"That is not enough," Chiverton said.

"Younger men might expect to propose on a weekly basis," McDonald lectured, "but, while that seems excessive, she can hardly be sure of your feelings if you do not express them regularly."

Ewan had not expected this. "I had not wished to be rebuffed..."

"... No one does," McDonald interrupted him. "If your intention is serious, you must risk it. Have you even written Miss Campbell poetry?"

"My valet felt that, given Miss Campbell's academic knowledge, she might not take my efforts seriously."

"That is irrelevant," McDonald said.

"I once wrote Alex a sonnet," Chiverton joined in. "We both

laughed over how bad it was, but I believe it helped ensure that Alex took my affections seriously."

Ewan frowned. He would have to study some of the better writers. "A sonnet..."

"I have a guinea for you in exchange for some simple information."

Standing next to a row of houses after carrying goods to a local merchant's home for a fee, Jed Cassell looked at the speaker with suspicion. The large, muscular man was Gabe Fryer and he was well-known for accepting money to rough people up. One man Gabe had beaten had nearly died and Jed had not realised Gabe was out of gaol yet. Any deal he wanted to make was likely to be over something Jed wanted nothing to do with. Besides that, the man stank as if he had not washed in months.

"What information?" he asked, keen to get the conversation over with.

Gabe grinned. It was not a pleasant expression and that was only partly because of his yellow, rotting teeth. "I just need to know who hired you to find out about Morag Duncan's death."

Jed's breath caught. The killer must have heard about his enquiries and feared being found. "Who wants to know that?"

"I do."

"You know what I mean. Perhaps I can pay better than your current employer."

"I doubt it," Gabe said with a snort of amusement.

So he was being paid a good deal. That revealed more than he'd likely intended. "You know I canna reveal who hired me. I'd lose my job as a caddie."

"I wouldna tell anyone where I got the information," Gabe promised. Jed had rarely heard a less reliable oath.

"Is this about Morag's criminal work? Are her former employers trying to hide their involvement?"

Gabe strode forward and, before Jed could even raise his fists, grabbed him by the neck. Jed was a strong man but he struggled ineffectively against the vice-like grip, panicking as fingers cut off his air supply. Gabe had approached him now for a reason: this street was too quiet for anyone to come to Jed's rescue.

"This would be a good time for you to change sides," the man said into his ear, as Jed continued to push frantically against the painful hold, his heart pounding and his vision blurring as he tried and failed to breathe in sufficient oxygen. "If you keep asking questions, your life may be as short as Morag's was. Tell your employer that this aint none of his business."

The choking grip on his neck vanished and Jed doubled over, gasping for air. The simple act of breathing in and out had never felt so good. By the time he recovered his breath and his wits, Fryer was gone.

Touching a hand to his throat, Jed got moving on shaky legs towards a high-quality part of the city: Mr MacPherson had to be told of this.

18. ROMANCE PROBLEMS

ISHBEL RETURNED home from a fascinating scientific lecture just in time to receive a visitor. Miss Chiverton wore a dress of the palest blue material that elegantly showed off her slender figure and brought out the deeper sky-blue of her eyes, but it was so flimsy and pale that Ishbel would have dismissed the cloth for herself as being too likely to show mud or ink-stains.

"I hope I have not ill-timed my call," Miss Chiverton said, following her into the house and removing her hat, which was in the same shade of blue as her dress. She brought with her the scent of lilacs but there was something strained about her air as she added, "I know that you have a great deal to occupy you."

Mr MacPherson was due to arrive soon but Miss Chiverton was unlikely to have any objection to his presence and they had no urgent demands on their morning. "Your timing is perfect. I am glad to see you again."

Miss Chiverton had once before wanted to turn their acquaintanceship into friendship but then the scandal about Ishbel's mother had been publicly revealed and Mrs Chiverton had kept her daughter away from Ishbel's company. Until now. Ishbel was happy to see her but wondered what had happened to cause the young woman to disobey her parents' wishes.

They handed their outdoor accoutrements to the butler and went into the drawing room, a footman following to close the window and add coal to the fire. Ishbel offered Miss Chiverton the chaise longue and sat down in a nearby upholstered chair.

"How is your new murder going?" Miss Chiverton asked, her intent expression suggesting that she did not notice her poor choice of words.

"We have not made a great deal of progress so far but it is necessary to be patient in such matters. We learn a great deal of information and then have to work out which is important, a little like playing chess without being able to see one's progress until the end of the game."

A second footman brought in their cups of chocolate. It was too early in the day for cakes, although Ishbel had been dressed for enough hours that she would have been glad of something to eat. They sat in a formal but friendly manner and delicately sipped their hot drinks, the rich, bitter taste of the chocolate proving fortifying to Ishbel.

"How is your cousin?" Miss Campbell asked.

"Very well." Ishbel was no good at these polite conversations but knew enough to respond to a question with a question. "How is your family?"

Miss Campbell put her cup down onto its saucer and stared at it. At length she said, "My oldest brother became engaged to be married at the end of last year and now Eddie has moved out of the house, so my parents have no one to focus their marital plans on save me."

"Oh, dear." Ishbel could think of nothing worse and, from Miss Campbell's unhappy expression, nor could she. "Is there anyone specific that they wish you to marry?"

"Not yet. I have received some... romantic interest since I came out into society." She paused and then her shoulders slumped and she gave an exasperated sigh. "I have turned down six offers of marriage so far."

"Six? That seems excessive!"

"Quite," Miss Campbell agreed with feeling. "If I knew how to put them off before they got to the proposal, I would. I was flattered at first, but one gentleman I have never had any liking for remains persistent and others appear on a weekly basis."

Ishbel took in Miss Chiverton's appearance and realised that she must seem like the ideal woman to a great many men. She had a rare beauty, polished manners and came from a wealthy, respectable family. That she possessed a good mind and the ability to see all that was superficial in the world around her were very likely qualities that eager courters would not even notice or would expect her to hide when she took on the role of wife.

Now that she recalled it, Ishbel had turned down three proposals herself in her first season and that was before she had even met Ewan. She had been too unsure of herself at seventeen and too aware that her decision not to marry would not be appreciated, to take any pleasure in the interest. Until she met Ewan and changed her mind about everything. Aware that Miss Chiverton seemed to be hoping for some form of advice from her, she belatedly suggested, "Perhaps you could carry a textbook wherever you go – I have found that this disturbs the majority of men."

Miss Campbell's eyes brightened. "I will do so."

They took a sip of their drinks in unison and the butler entered the room to announce Mr MacPherson's arrival. The women put their cups and saucers down on the coffee tables situated close by for this purpose and stood up as Mr MacPherson walked in. Ishbel and Miss Campbell curtsied as Mr MacPherson bowed to each of them and Ishbel found herself taking in his engaging smile as if seeing him anew.

He sat down with them and made polite conversation, asking all the correct questions to Miss Campbell, but Ishbel could tell that something was troubling him and, as they caught each other's eye and a look of understanding passed between them, she waited for them to be alone, so she could find out what was wrong.

19. FIRST SIGN OF DANGER

"I MUST admit that this information is unsettling," Ishbel said, after Miss Chiverton left, when Mr MacPherson told her what happened to Jed. "Is Mr Cassell hurt?"

"No. He says he is unharmed and more determined than ever to help us solve this matter."

"Good." She found herself liking the young caddie more than ever, although she was concerned for his safety, alone on the Edinburgh streets at all hours. "The person who hired this criminal to talk to Mr Cassell does not know who we are, so we are in no danger for the moment. It is frustrating to think that the ruffian probably knew the name of Morag's killer."

"Jed told me that the man is a long-time criminal who was clearly being paid a lot not to reveal anything about his employer. There would be no use in approaching him and it might bring danger down on us."

"This proves that Morag's death was not the result of a theft," she said.

Mr MacPherson's expression was distracted as he agreed with her. "Ishbel, I know how much your freedom means to you, but would you have a footman accompany you whenever you leave the house alone? We gave our names to some of the shopkeepers when we asked about Morag, so it is only a matter of time before our identities are known by this criminal. It would be easy for someone to harm or threaten you."

He had not called her by her first name since before their estrangement and it was pleasant, more so than perhaps was warranted, to hear him do so now. She disliked what he was suggesting but could see that the wisdom in the idea. "Very well.

Just until any peril is gone."

"Thank you."

"I trust you will be careful too."

He smiled. "I shall."

"Until we hear more from Mr Cassell, I am not sure how we should proceed with our enquiries."

"Nor I."

"Then perhaps we should consider what we have learnt so far." When he agreed to this she went and fetched her notes on the matter and said, "Morag Duncan, a young working-class woman, was killed on the Thursday of last week in an alley not far removed from the heart of the city. We do not know why she was there but it is possible that it had to do with some criminal activity. She was killed in what the Town Guards are assuming was a robbery but we have established that this conclusion is wrong. Also, a guinea coin was left behind."

She paused and Mr MacPherson took over the summary. "She had been a thief when she was a child, stealing from a woman at the factory where she worked." In a different tone he said, "Would it be useful to look further into the theft? Could Morag have had a grudge against the woman she stole from?"

"It was a very long time ago," Ishbel said. "Unless someone forced her to commit the theft, I do not believe it could have any relevance to what she did after that."

"Could there have been someone we have not heard about who compelled her to steal? We have assumed that she had turned away from crime until George Smith tempted her back to it, but what if there was someone else all along?"

Ishbel considered this. "Her parents seemed genuinely upset over the past theft. Her father was angry at the idea of her being involved in anything illegal and the lawyer, Lord Tain, said that her parents had been shocked over what Morag had done. She has no other family on her father's side but we know nothing of other relations." She stood up once more. "I will ask Lucy to join us. She will know more on the subject."

She found her lady's maid upstairs and explained their idea as she brought her down to the drawing room. Lucy curtsied to Mr MacPherson and, with clear uncertainty over the decorum of such a thing, sat down with them.

"I met Morag's grandparents a few times," Lucy said, "but I believe only her father's mother is still alive – Mr Duncan's mother, that is, not her real father. I never heard a word said about there being any criminals amongst their relations and children hear a lot that would not be spoken of in front of adults. Mrs Duncan has a married sister who lives close by but I really think that Mr and Mrs Duncan would have disowned anyone who did anything illegal, particularly anyone who might have been a bad influence on Morag after the factory robbery. Both of them are God-fearing and being respectable matters a lot to them, particularly Mr Duncan."

Ishbel recalled the man who had been furious at the idea that Morag might have stolen the guinea found with her and Mrs Duncan saying that anger was his way of dealing with the grief. She thought that Lucy was most likely correct in her assessment of them. "Did she have any other friends in her childhood who she could have kept in touch with?"

"There was one other girl who grew up in the same street as us. Her name was..." She squinted at the far wall before saying, "... Lottie. I remember her saying that she was named after the queen, as if it made her better than the rest of us. She and I dinna take to each other – I found some of her comments too mean-spirited – but Morag liked her. Lottie was a year younger than us and admired Morag, enjoying hearing about her dreams for a happier future. I dinna ken if they stayed friends, though. I can tell you where she lives, or at least where her parents lived, if you want to speak to her."

Ishbel considered the suggestion and said, "It can do no harm."

20. MORAG'S LIFE

LOTTIE JONES was now Lottie Miller and had three young children, whom she curtly banished upstairs when Ewan and Miss Campbell called. She had light brown hair cut in a modern style with short curls around her face and green eyes highlighted by the deep green morning dress she wore, that was cut in a fashionable but severe style.

Lottie added another log to the fire and made tea for them all, although it was early in the day for the drink, and they sat in a rough circle around a medium-sized table in the parlour, sun lighting up the room from a large window. "Dear Morag and Lucy," she said, feigning the English accent that was spoken by most of the upper classes, her tone perfunctory, "we were such good friends. I was heartbroken to hear of Morag's death."

"Did you keep in touch with Morag much after she left her parents' home to begin working, Mrs Miller?" Ishbel asked.

Lottie studied her with shrewd eyes and answered in that deliberate, quiet tone. "Yes, of course. We met every month or so to talk."

"Your family did not worry about the fact that she had been accused of theft?"

"I did not tell them. I felt Morag particularly needed my friendship after that unhappy incident. They found out eventually and warned me to shun her but I didn't. It was one mistake and she regretted it bitterly."

"Why was that?" Ishbel asked.

Lottie raised an eyebrow. "It nearly ruined her life, Miss Campbell. If she'd been taken to court who knows what the punishment might have been?" There was something in her tone that was at odds with her words, as if she had taken some enjoyment in hearing of such dark events. Ishbel could already see why Lucy, who was straightforward and kind-hearted, had never liked her.

"What was her life like after that?"

"Her father managed to get another job for her, something similarly tedious and exhausting. She stuck at it for about a year and then found another job that she liked better. Mr Duncan wasn't happy about it, but he accepted that at least she was still working hard."

"Then it must have annoyed him that she had no employment recently," Ishbel said.

"Oh, yes. They argued about it a lot. I told her that she should find herself a good husband – I'd met Mr Miller by then and, as you can see, I have a very comfortable life."

Since it seemed to be expected, Ishbel said, "Your house is lovely." She had seen enough working-class homes to recognise that this was one of the better ones, small but possessing furniture of a reasonable quality and if Lottie did not have to take on a job at all, in addition to raising her children, then she was fortunate. This room was also kept in immaculate condition. Ishbel would have found it hard to believe that there were any children in the house if she had not seen them herself. There was not even any noise from upstairs to indicate their presence.

Lottie seemed delighted by the compliment. "Mr Miller has an excellent job working in a fashionable shop. He is often left in full charge of it."

"That must be very pleasant for you both," Ishbel said and looked over at Mr MacPherson.

He took her silent hint and got the conversation back to the reason they were here. "Was Morag still living with family friends at that time?"

"Yes. She stayed with them for four or five years. They had older children of their own and I believe it was nice for them to have a younger child to look after, although of course Morag was out working a lot of the time."

"I presume they were people of good character?"

"Very respectable," Lottie told them. "I think they attended the same church as Mr and Mrs Duncan."

"And their children were the same?"

"I suppose so. If you are wondering if any of them encouraged Morag to steal, then I think not. They only had one unmarried daughter left at home when Morag started living there and they didn't get on well at all. Morag would never have stolen in order to win her goodwill. No, I think it was a silly impulse to steal the money. I imagine Morag thought of all the pretty things she could buy and never considered what would happen if she was caught. She certainly thought about it afterwards, though. When she told me all about it, she was shaking at the thought she could have been imprisoned. I'll never forget the look of terror on her face." Once again there was a hint of relish in her voice over what Morag had suffered.

"Then why would she risk her life again?" Ishbel asked.

"Was she doing that?" Lottie did not look shocked. "I wondered how she got her money lately, but she wouldn't admit anything. If she was in trouble again, she was doing it for the same reason as most young women do foolish things. Love."

21. REASONS FOR MURDER

LOTTIE MILLER looked pleased to find that her words had got their full attention.

Ewan wondered why his instincts told him not to accept everything she said as the absolute truth. Lottie was attractive, although not in a way that stood out from other women, and dressed neatly, a bright ribbon in her hair to suggest that her looks were still important to her. There was something cold about her attitude, though, that showed in the stern way she had controlled her children, and she was clearly keen to do all she could to improve her standing in the world. She adopted a different accent to impress them and her words about her husband suggested that she would not relax until he had the most successful job possible.

"Who was Morag in love with?" Miss Campbell asked, outshining Lottie in every way without trying. It was like comparing the glory of the sun to a shadow.

"Why, George Smith, of course. He told her he loved her and wanted them to have a grand life but it was obvious that he wasn't sincere."

"How?" Ewan asked.

"After months of living under the same roof, they were not engaged. She believed every piece of flattery he paid her, the silly girl. She wouldn't listen to any of my warnings or advice and, beneath the compliments and crooked smile, George Smith was nothing more than a cheap criminal."

"Do you think he could have hurt her?" Ishbel asked, frowning.

"Perhaps."

"When was the last time that you saw Morag?" Ewan asked.

Lottie considered this for perhaps longer than was warranted, still enjoying having her wealthy guests paying her so much attention. "It would have been just under two weeks ago."

That would have been just before the visit to her parents. "How did she seem to you?" he said. "Happy? Worried?"

Lottie's brow furrowed. "Nervous."

"About what?" Ishbel asked.

"She wouldn't tell me. She kept saying it was nothing but she was fidgeting and distracted."

"What did you converse about?"

"My life and hers. George, and how they would be so happy together. Actually, there was something odd. She asked if I loved my children and if all parents loved their children. When I said yes, it seemed to put her in a better mood."

"Her family told us that Morag asked about her father when she last saw them."

"But he's dead, isn't he?" Lottie said. "Why would that have anything to do with her death? I thought... well, I hate to even suggest such a terrible thing of a friend, but I wondered if she was expecting a child."

She had lowered her voice to a whisper and Ewan could only just make out the words. He paused to consider them. If George had never intended to marry her, how would he react to hearing such news?

"Do you think George might have killed Morag?" Ewan asked when he and Miss Campbell were alone in the library of her house, surrounded by the sight and smell of books.

"It seems unlikely," Miss Campbell said, surprising him.

"Surely he is the most likely person to have committed the deed?"

"In an alley where he might have been caught? With a knife that would have covered him in blood? She lived in his house. If he had wanted her dead he could have found a safer way to do it."

He had not considered this. "But if she told him she was with child, might he not have panicked and got rid of her by the quickest means?"

"Why? She could not force him to marry her. He was already a criminal, so I doubt he would care about treating a young woman shamefully. Besides, this is a guess on Lottie Miller's part and she might not have been correct. There are many reasons that Morag might have been dwelling on the subject of family. She might have feared that her parents would find out she was involved in crimes again. She might have been looking for more information about her father or his family."

"But neither of those concerns would be likely to have led to her death."

"She mixed with criminals. To me, that seems by far the most likely reason for her death and the guinea coin she had suggests being paid for something illegal."

It was likely that Miss Campbell was correct, although the subject of a possible baby stayed in his mind. "Then I think we will have to rely on Jed to find out more about that. She had been involved in selling stolen items for a time, though, so I wonder what happened recently to make Mrs Miller think she was nervous."

22. AN UNSCRUPULOUS MAN

EWAN TORE up another sheet of paper and let his quill hover over a fresh one. He had not expected this to be quite so difficult. Part of the problem was that he was not sure how Miss Campbell would react to unexpectedly receiving poetry from him and he feared that a badly written sonnet would lessen her opinion of him rather than the reverse. Both Chiverton and McDonald had felt strongly that he should be more active in his courtship of Miss Campbell, though, and, on consideration, he thought that they were right. If he was not sure of her feelings, how could she be certain of his?

He resolutely dipped his quill in the pot of sepia ink and looked down at the dauntingly blank page. After some seconds, a blob of ink dripped onto the paper, necessitating yet another fresh start. If he kept on like this he would run out of paper.

Ewan's butler walked in, an annoyed look in his deeply set eyes. "There is a Mr Cassell here to see you, sir. Are you at home to him?"

Ewan put down his quill and stood up. "I will be glad to speak to him."

He followed MacCuaig into the hall and greeted Jed, inviting him into the drawing room.

"What have you discovered?" he asked, waving the muscular young man towards a chair. Jed waited until Ewan was seated before following suit, as always looking uncomfortable in an affluent environment.

"George Smith has a reputation for treating the lassies badly, Mr MacPherson. He makes promises of marriage and a fine life that he has no intention of keeping, encouraging the women into worse and worse crimes. One of his lovers even sold her body, with him said to keep most of the money she made, until he discarded her for a younger, fresher lass. It's believed that he also forced his sister into pick-pocketing and, later, more daring thefts – he has her completely under his control. It's only good luck that neither of them's been arrested yet."

"Or bad luck for Morag." The news confirmed Ishbel's opinion that George would have had little reason to care, let alone kill Morag, for bearing his child, if that had indeed happened.

"Miss Duncan had spent a lot of money in the last couple of weeks. Either she'd been involved in a much bigger crime than before or she was being paid generously by someone for something. I couldna discover more than it. Also, Gabe Fryer has been causing more trouble," Jed told him and Ewan listened intently. "Several people were given bribes not to tell us anything more about Morag Duncan. It seems that Fryer managed to find someone to tell him your name and Miss Campbell's. No one's been paid to do anything violent, though; I checked that."

"Then Miss Campbell is not in any danger? None of us are?"

The younger man's keen eyes and thin mouth drooped downwards. "I canna say for sure, sir. All I know is that someone wealthy dinna want the two of you to find out anything about Morag's death. If I hear anything else I'll let you know."

"Thank you, Jed."

Ewan paid him for the work he had done and Jed left him to his thoughts and to another attempt at sonnet writing.

23. DENIAL

"THE FACTS Mr Cassell has uncovered lead us back to George Smith and the work he had Morag doing," Ishbel said, putting her gloves on. They were walking in the formal garden behind the house, the garden no more than greenery at this time of year before any of the flowers began to blossom, although there was a pleasant fragrance from the herbs.

"Yes, and I have been thinking about the money she had," Mr MacPherson said. He slowed his long strides to keep pace with her, the red frock coat and matching breeches he wore today giving him a regal look. "You recall that Lottie Miller said she had told Morag that George was not treating her honestly?"

"Very clearly. I got the impression that Morag usually listened to Lottie and that she was annoyed that Morag was so much under George's influence."

"But what if Morag had begun to take Lottie's words seriously? That could be why she had more money recently, that she had stopped sharing it with George, and she might have been nervous because she wanted to get away from him."

"That is very possible," she said, part of her mind enjoying the dappled light that fell beneath a pear tree, while the rest of her concentration was on the problem, "and if he thought she was cheating him out of money he felt he was entitled to, that might be enough reason for him to murder her."

"He could have confronted her in the street about the guinea she had on her and, when she admitted the truth, he might have killed her in the passion of the moment."

They had learnt during their last criminal matter that people sometimes felt the need to keep knives with them for protection. In

George Smith's case, he might have carried a weapon for a darker reason. "Your theory is certainly plausible. I think we should see Smith again at once."

"Yes."

She began to walk towards the path to the front of the house and realised he was not following. When she turned back to face him, there was an odd look on his face and something hesitant in his manner. "Is something wrong?"

"No." He cleared his throat. "Not at all. This is something I wrote for you."

He stepped forward and she took the sealed note he held out, breaking the wax and opening it. She had expected it to be something to do with the case and so she did not immediately understand what she was looking at, but then she realised. He had written a sonnet about her. She read it slowly. It was not flowery or elaborate but there was a beauty in the turn of phrase he used and it showed that he saw her in a way she had never imagined anyone could, as someone extraordinary.

"I am no great writer..." He began uncomfortably.

"... It is lovely," she interrupted him. "I am very glad to receive it." Her own words were failing her now but, as his gaze met hers, she hoped he could tell how much she was moved by this gesture of affection.

They walked out to the pavement and she let Mr MacPherson take her gloved hand to help her into his carriage, the touch making her skin tingle. She remained composed with difficulty. He still loved her. She had not been certain and the fear that she had destroyed his feelings with her clumsy behaviour had haunted her.

The carriage came to a measured halt in front of the building where Smith had a flat. The cobbled street around them looked grubbier in the sunlight than it had in the rain, the houses discoloured and unkempt, weeds pushing through the stones and piles of unwholesome debris lying in corners. The odour was also foul, a mixture of human and animal waste from the horse manure in the roads and the contents of chamber pots thrown out of windows.

They entered the unlocked door and walked up narrow stairs, rats scurrying away at the sight of them. Mr MacPherson knocked sharply upon Smith's door and, after a minute, footsteps sounded and the man opened it. He looked taken aback at the sight of them and none too pleased. He reluctantly admitted them to the main room, which was as squalid as ever, with half-eaten food lying about and damp stains on a corner of the ceiling. There was no sign of his sister.

"I told you all I knew about Morag," he said, folding his arms. He was only half-dressed, wearing shirt and breeches but without waistcoat, jacket or neck-cloth, so more of his chest was revealed than was decent in front of a lady.

"Hardly," Ewan disagreed. "We know that you involved her in criminal work, selling on possessions that you stole."

Smith's dark eyes widened and darted from one to the other of them. "You canna accuse me of such things."

"I think that you killed Morag," Mr MacPherson went on. "I think you suspected she was keeping money from you. Perhaps she wanted to leave here."

"She never," he said with a return of his former arrogant confidence. "She wanted to marry me. She was desperate for someone to show her a life that was more than just hard work that would one day kill her."

"Then where did she get the guinea that was found on her when she died?"

"A guinea?" His surprise looked unfeigned. "That's impossible. Look, I might not have been as fond of Morag as she was of me, but she was my sister's friend and we were both upset over her death. If you still dinna believe me, then just ask at the Fox tavern. I was dicing and drinking there with friends and came home to hear that she'd just been killed."

"We will check this information."

"Do what you want," Smith growled, stepping close to Mr MacPherson in a menacing stance, "but dinna come back here. I've had more than enough out of you."

24. THOUGHTS ON MARRIAGE

IF SHE and Mr MacPherson had thought that George Smith might be lying about where he was when Morag died, they were soon proven wrong. The tavern owner and several customers remembered him being there, the date standing out with them as they had all heard about Morag's murder. The statements ended any possibility that Smith could be the killer, which was a blow since they had no other real suspect.

It was approaching the hour when luncheon was served in Ishbel's house – a meal she usually missed due to her academic schedule and other pastimes – so she invited Mr MacPherson to join her family. Harriette and Lord Huntly were used to Ewan's company by now and treated him with an easy familiarity which, where Harriette was concerned, meant a great many sarcastic comments. For the first time, Ishbel dared to imagine joining such a gathering where she and Ewan were married and the pleasure this idea caused was almost overwhelming.

When the meal was over, she and Mr MacPherson removed to the library to discuss how to pursue their murder enquiry now that their main suspect was found to be innocent. They both remained standing, moving around the spacious room as they considered what they had learned.

"I believe we have not just exonerated George Smith but also his criminal friends," she said. "After all, if Morag had been killed because of her illegal activities, surely Mr Smith would be in danger too since they were equally involved in them? He has not shown the slightest fear for his safety in front of us."

"Morag could have been involved in something that he was not aware of. He seemed shocked to hear about the money she had on her when she died."

"Yes, we should certainly try to find out where it came from," she agreed, picking up a book from the table in front of her and absently returning it to its correct place on the shelves. "Also, I am not certain how it could be relevant but I keep thinking of Morag's questions about her real father. I believe I will send out letters requesting his name from her mother's Marriage Certificate."

"We could just ask Mrs Duncan."

"Mr Duncan, we have been told, is a jealous man and this is probably nothing to do with our enquiry, so I would not like to bother the family for no reason while they are grieving. Even if the father had relations still alive, I can think of no reason for them to harm Morag. It is just something we know she was preoccupied with before she died."

"Then who should we question next?" Mr MacPherson asked, leaning against the marble mantelpiece. "It seems as if our enquiry has come to a halt."

"Morag's throat was cut. We agreed that her death would have been a messy one. I find it difficult to believe that no one saw a person whose hands, if not clothes, were covered in blood. I did not show you the alley where she died but both ends of it turned into busy streets."

"I will speak to Jed and ask him to make enquiries about it."

She suspected that Mr Cassell had already done this, as by now he knew as much as they did about what facts were useful in such matters. If no one had already come forward with such information, perhaps they were too afraid to do so.

After Mr MacPherson left, Ishbel went looking for Lucy, who was in the kitchen mending the hem of one of Ishbel's dresses.

"How can I help, miss?" Lucy asked when Ishbel said that she needed information for their enquiry.

"Would you be able to find out Mrs Duncan's Christian name and maiden name for me? I do not wish to trouble her directly for it unless I have to."

"I've heard a few people use her first name – it's Beth. And my family attended the wedding of Mrs Duncan's sister. Before she was wed, she was Miss Emily Grey, so Grey would have been Mrs Duncan's maiden name too."

"That is perfect. Thank you." Ishbel went on to let her know that their suspicion of George Smith had got nowhere but that they were still working on the matter and Lucy seemed happy with this.

Ishbel then walked from the servants' wing up to the main house and then up the larger staircase to her bed chamber. She sat at her desk and, since she did not know which church Mrs Duncan had been married in, she wrote a letter to all the churches in Edinburgh asking for information from Elizabeth Grey's Marriage Certificate.

She then opened her reticule, got out the parchment contained in it and re-read the sonnet Ewan had written for her.

25. ANNOUNCEMENT

MATILDA AND her family were due to arrive in Edinburgh today, so Ewan invited a few of his acquaintances to his house for an informal tea party. In truth, it was an excuse created for the purpose of introducing Ishbel to his family.

He spent the morning supervising the household arrangements for his family's arrival, managing to thoroughly annoy his butler, MacCuaig, who had had the work entirely under control. Ewan was excited to see his family but also extremely aware that he did not live the kind of life they would wish him to. He had always been able to talk easily to his sister, though, and would need to rely on her to handle her husband, whose old-fashioned opinions Ewan clearly recalled.

Ishbel was the first person to arrive at his home, escorted by Lord and Lady Huntly. Ewan had realised he could not invite Ishbel without her family, but he was not confident that Lady Huntly's forthright views would be appreciated by Picton or even Matilda. His plan was that, after making the introductions between them all, he would spend the next hour keeping them as far away from each other as possible.

Chiverton then arrived with his sister, Miss Chiverton, his older brother, Henry, and his brother's fiancée, Miss Anne Castlebrook. McDonald's carriage drew up to the house just behind theirs. Everyone had dressed in smart clothes for the occasion, the men in bright colours, their neck-cloths tied in elegantly designed knots, while Lady Huntly, the only married woman present, wore an elaborate sky-blue gown with a velvet mantelet – a short cape – and feathered hat. The unmarried ladies wore pale dresses and Ishbel was particularly lovely in a gown that had small pink embroidered flowers on it, her hair a mass of copper curls beneath her shepherdess hat and her delicate features slightly flushed. Ewan could hardly bear to look away from her.

A footman handed out drinks as the guests talked to each other and, even half distracted by what lay ahead, Ewan could not help but notice which people conversed easily to each other, who disliked whom and who was nervous. While several people avoided getting into conversation with Lady Huntly, Miss Castlebrook listened to her every word with awe and admiration.

While the others were occupied, Ewan and Ishbel wandered out of hearing distance and Ishbel said quietly, "I do hope your sister will think well of me. Would you remind me what are the names of your nephew and nieces?"

"Rebecca, James and baby Anne. I am certain my family will be enchanted by you, although I wish I could introduce you to her as my fiancée," Ewan said without thinking and was then horrified with himself for such a blunder. He had not only ruined the opportunity to make an elegant proposal but had also spoken in an unfair way about their relationship.

Ishbel took in his expression and said calmly, "Then you should do so."

He stared at her. "I beg your pardon?"

She gave a wide smile, her eyes shining. "Nothing would give me more happiness than to become your wife, Ewan."

"Good. I... May I..."

"Yes," she said, so he leaned forward and kissed her. It was meant to be the kind of polite kiss that was appropriate to such a situation but they rather forgot themselves. And the fact that the rest of Ewan's guests were able to see them.

They hastily unwound their arms from each other's person as Lady Huntly said dryly, "I trust this means that you have an announcement to make?"

Ishbel put her hand on his arm and, brimming over with happiness, Ewan said, "Miss Campbell has consented to accept my hand in marriage."

"Finally!" Lady Huntly said but she was smiling as she spoke.

They headed back to the group at the same time as Chiverton and McDonald approached to hug Ewan and congratulate him. Miss Chiverton likewise embraced Ishbel as the men continued to slap

Ewan on the back and express their pleasure.

"Mr MacPherson," a voice said and Ewan turned to his butler who told the assembled group, "Lord Picton, Lady Picton, Miss Rebecca, Miss Anne and Master James."

Ewan had not heard the carriage arrive, nor the front door open in all the excitement. His sister and her husband entered the room with their three young children, the baby resting in Matilda's arms. Ewan strode across to them and said, "Welcome to my home. This is the happiest of days."

He kissed Matilda's forehead and exchanged a fond smile with her, then shook Picton's hand, noting that the man's hair had a touch of grey at the temples now. Picton had never been a dashing man but he had an air of authority and Matilda had found him good-hearted and reliable. Ewan crouched down to hug and kiss Becca and Jamie before straightening and touching the cheek of the sleepy baby. The older children had a look of Matilda in their eyes and smiles but Ewan could not yet tell who the baby would resemble.

"This is Anne, your newest niece," Matilda told him before saying to the infant, "and this is your Uncle Ewan."

The baby waved her tiny hands and he watched her with a smile, grateful that he would have the chance to see her grow up. Perhaps in a few years Anne might even have a baby cousin to play games with and the thought made his smile grow.

"If you are not too fatigued from the journey may I introduce my guests to you, those you have not already met? I thought you might enjoy informal refreshments with a few of my closest acquaintances and my cook made some sweetmeats for the children to enjoy."

"That sounds lovely," Matilda said. She had changed little in the years they had been apart, although he had grown taller while growing to manhood, making the difference in their heights more marked. She had the same wide green eyes as he did but had inherited their father's darker hair. Although she was a mature wife and mother now of two score years and three, he could still see the girl who had played outside with him, told him stories and comforted him after their mother died.

Ewan turned to Ishbel, smiling at her and receiving a warm look in return. Although they did not have a great deal in common, he felt sure that his sister and Ishbel would like each other. "This is Miss Campbell, who has today done me the immeasurable honour of agreeing to become my wife."

Matilda's expression hardened as Ishbel walked forward and curtsied to her.

There was a pause where Matilda should have returned the gesture and did not, and that was the instant when Ewan began to feel uneasy. The light conversation between the other guests tailed off as all eyes turned towards the women, who were still facing each other.

Matilda finally responded to Ewan's statement in a quiet but firm manner: "I think not."

26. A HUMILIATING SITUATION

JED STOOD on the crowded High Street and handed out pamphlets advertising a new shop to anyone who would take one. He was worn out, having worked half the night too, but he needed the extra money. His youngest brother was finally recovering from a long illness that his whole family had feared would kill him, but the care and treatment of a physician had cost a fortune, more than most people of his class could pay. Jed had refused to do nothing and watch him die, telling his parents and older siblings that he would be responsible for paying the fee, but it was a struggle to pay the monthly amount. Without the generosity of Miss Campbell and Mr MacPherson he never could have managed it.

He heard someone call his name over the shouting of the street sellers and clatter of horses' hooves, and looked around, to see his friend and fellow caddie, Billy, jog over to him, a frown on his freckled face instead of the usual smile.

"I was asking about the Morag Duncan murder for you," Billy said in an undertone, while Jed continued to give the sheets of paper to passersby. "It turns out that I wasna the only one and someone threatened to beat me up unless I left the matter alone."

"Was it Gabe Fryer who said this?"

"No, a couple of other men. Known criminals. The violent types."

How many people had been hired? The person in charge either had a lot of money to throw about or they knew a lot of criminals. He would guess at the latter. It made him wonder if Morag had been involved in something far bigger than he had discovered so far. No one went to this much trouble over a small-time thief.

"Are you all right?" he asked.

"Yeah. They dinna do nothing, but someone really dinna want Morag's murder solved."

"Was anything at all said about who hired them? Even a hint?"

"No," Billy said, smiling at a pretty woman in a large, feathered hat as she took one of the pamphlets. He clearly wasn't too shaken by his earlier encounter. The lady ignored him and, as she strolled off, he gave his attention back to Jed. "You need to be careful, maybe even stop working on this matter, because these ruffians are dangerous. I dinna want you getting killed too."

"I'm not backing off but I promise I'll keep to the busy streets and not turn my back on anyone rough-looking." It wasn't as if this was the first time he'd helped catch a criminal and he knew how to take care of himself.

"That's probably what Morag Duncan told herself," Billy said, his eyes shadowed with worry before he walked away.

Jed was too busy thinking over what this information revealed to give any serious thought to the additional danger.

Ishbel stayed silent, not knowing how to respond to Lady Picton's words. Her cheeks burned at the snub as she turned back towards her family. To know that someone so close to Ewan thought so little of her was worse than anything said or implied by Edinburgh's ton. Harriette put an arm round her shoulders, eyes flashing with fury, and Lord Huntly's normally amiable face held a frown.

Ewan whispered something to his sister, who shook her head, expression unbending. He shot a glance at Ishbel in which she saw her own hurt and mortification reflected and then, since he could hardly send the other guests away, he was forced to introduce the other people to his family as if nothing was amiss. Chiverton and McDonald already seemed acquainted with Ewan's sister and Ishbel remembered that they had been friends with him since childhood, so they would have known all his family. She gathered that they had also met Lord Picton, although they seemed to have little to say to him. No one had much to say in this uncomfortable atmosphere.

Ewan muttered something in the ear of Mr Chiverton, who nodded and engaged Lord Picton in conversation, drawing the rest of the group into his circle. Ewan then led his sister to one side. Before Ishbel could stop her, Harriette marched over to them. Fearful of what her cousin might say, Ishbel drew closer to unobtrusively eavesdrop, ready to step between the women and lead Harriette away if an argument broke out.

"I am Lady Huntly and Miss Campbell is my cousin," Harriette said in the tone of one of society's leaders, someone who could elevate or crush a person with a few well-chosen words.

"I have heard of you," Lady Picton said in a respectful voice, "and know that no stain can possibly fall on you or your husband, but your cousin's mother is infamous..."

"That is nothing to do with Ishbel. She came to live with Lord Huntly and me when she was still a child and I trust you will find no fault with that arrangement."

"I am not so hard-hearted that I would hold her mother's immoral behaviour against Miss Campbell if she comported herself in a respectable manner. However, I am informed by friends that she does not."

Ishbel could not bear to hear any more of what had been said against her so she joined Mr Chiverton's group. Her breath was shallow, her limbs shaky and she could not bring herself to meet the eyes of the other people, horrified at the idea of what must be going through their minds at this time.

Miss Chiverton took her gloved hand. "Do you think spring is on its way, Miss Campbell? The milder weather of the last few days has been quite invigorating."

"Yes." She swallowed and gratefully focused on the fair-haired woman. "I hope so. It has been a harsh winter."

Mr McDonald joined in. "We must put together a party next month for a picnic."

"That sounds delightful." Ishbel smiled at him but her body tensed again as Ewan, Harriette and Lady Picton re-joined the main group. Harriette's fierce expression told its own story and Ewan looked just as angry. Lady Picton moved to stand next to her husband, body turned slightly away from her brother. The children's governess had taken charge of the children who were enjoying the cakes and lemonade, too young to recognise that anything was wrong.

"MacPherson," Mr McDonald said, "where do you think would be an enjoyable location for a picnic?"

Ewan gave a strained smile. "There are many pleasant areas

outside the city. Perhaps somewhere with a view of the coast?"

The tea party continued in the same manner, with superficial conversation failing to hide the tension between half of those present, and at the same impossibly slow pace. By the time her family took their leave of Ewan, it felt to Ishbel as if she had experienced a lifetime of embarrassment here.

Ewan took her hand and squeezed it, positioning his body to hide what he was doing from the others present. "I will resolve this with my family," he said to her in an undertone, "and everything will be well. I love you."

These words almost caused her to break into tears on the spot. She looked into his eyes and let herself believe all that he had said.

After all that their relationship had survived, she needed to have faith that it was not over now.

27. ARGUMENT

"HOW COULD you treat the woman I love in such a cruel manner?" Ewan demanded.

The guests were gone and the governess had taken the children and the baby upstairs to rest. He was left in the drawing room with Matilda and Lord Picton, she seated near the fire while her husband stood beside her chair with Ewan standing opposite them, close to the door.

"I do not appreciate you speaking to my wife in that manner," Picton said.

"Then you can understand my anger and hurt over the way Ishbel was spoken to." Ewan glared at them both, barely able to believe that a sister who loved him could behave in such a way.

"Ewan," Matilda said in the gentle tone she had used when they were younger, one that was painful to hear in these circumstances, "I would be remiss in my duty as your older sibling were I to sanction a match between you and someone so lacking in all propriety."

"Matilda, it has been a considerable time since I was a child, so it is not your place to choose my bride for me, nor to argue with my choice. Also, since when were you so lacking in good sense that you would base your entire opinion of someone on cheap gossip?"

His sister stiffened at the rebuke and Picton intervened again. "That is going too far, MacPherson."

Matilda looked up at her husband. "I wish to answer, Gregory." When he put a hand on her shoulder and nodded, she turned back to Ewan. "I very much regret causing Miss Campbell any grief but everything I have heard, even from you – speaking of her as your partner in resolving problems – goes against her. Your announcement of an engagement forced me to make my feelings clear about such a thing while there is still time to put an end to this liaison."

"Nothing could induce me to break my engagement to Ishbel."

Matilda raised her chin. "You would ruin the good reputation of your own family by forcing such an unsavoury association upon us?"

Ewan opened his mouth to give the response to this accusation that it deserved, but Picton spoke first. "This has been a long, tiring day for everyone. I think we will be able to reach a more satisfactory outcome to such a conversation tomorrow when everyone is less emotional."

Matilda agreed to this with a look of such relief that Ewan felt a stab of guilt at distressing her, even though his anger and worry for Ishbel and their relationship remained strong. He realised how close he and his sister were to an estrangement when, given the chance to get to know Ishbel for herself, Matilda might be persuaded to change her opinion.

"Yes," Ewan said, grateful for Picton's intervention. "Perhaps that would be for the best."

He left them alone and went for a walk to calm himself down. He wondered how Ishbel was feeling and it hurt to think that his own family had put her through such a painful ordeal. When she had agreed to marry him he had thought their lives would be transformed, that nothing would seem difficult or unpleasant ever again. They had both been happy.

Perhaps he should have foreseen this and written Matilda long letters telling her all about Ishbel's virtues, of which there were many, but it had never occurred to him that his sister would react in such a way, as if his own feelings meant nothing compared to a handful of people decrying the match. He thought back to Matilda's own entry into society – she had certainly shown a more perfect version of herself, sensitive to the thought of any negative pronouncements being made about her character, but she had barely been an adult at the time, so such a reaction was understandable. He had assumed that her marriage would allow her to view the world around her in a more considered manner, caring more about her family than the opinions of strangers. Perhaps that was at the heart of her fears: the idea that her husband would criticise her for Ewan's actions. But Picton had not said a word against Ishbel. At least, not in Ewan's hearing.

He no longer knew what to think, save that he would let nothing and no one come between himself and Ishbel.

Ewan managed to have a civil conversation with Matilda and Picton over dinner, mainly by focusing on the subject of the children. He wanted to know all about their lives and the stilted manners at the start of the meal faded as everyone expressed genuine enthusiasm over letting the children get to know Edinburgh.

The next morning, after passing a sleepless night thinking and re-thinking what to say, he asked to speak to Matilda privately after breakfast. They went outside to talk, Ewan hoping that the tranquil setting would allow for a calmer conversation.

Matilda spoke first. "I very much regret the events of yesterday. You clearly have strong feelings for Miss Campbell and I do not wish there to be a rift between us."

"Nor do I," he said, breathing more easily at these words.

"Would you postpone the public announcement of your engagement to Miss Campbell to allow me a bit of time to get to know her?"

That was hardly the direction he had hoped her words were moving in. "Matilda, I very much wish for you to become acquainted with Ishbel, but can you not accept my word that she is a good person? After what happened yesterday I would hate for those who were already told of our engagement to believe I had been persuaded to distance myself from Ishbel."

"I am sure your friends will understand how important it is for your family to properly make the acquaintance of Miss Campbell. Otherwise I cannot in good conscience support the match."

"I will speak to Ishbel about what you have said," he reluctantly told her, hating the fact that he could not immediately reassure Ishbel that he had changed his sister's mind. "The final decision on how to progress will be hers."

28. ISHBEL AGREES TO A COMPROMISE

ISHBEL KNEW as soon as she saw Ewan, the morning after his sister's arrival, that Lady Picton's opinion of Ishbel remained the same.

He told her what Matilda had said. "I wish I knew a way to instantly show her all your wonderful qualities."

Ishbel suspected that Lady Picton hoped that a postponement of the engagement would give her a chance to end the relationship. Seen from Lady Picton's point of view, Ishbel could not even blame her for feeling Ishbel was unworthy of Ewan. Ishbel was aware of the irregular nature of her life when compared to that of some lady of spotless reputation that Ewan might instead marry. She knew too that had she only resolved her doubts about marriage sooner, she and Ewan might already be publicly engaged by now, when it would be too late for Lady Picton to stop it without causing more scandal. Her current unhappiness was, therefore, partly of her own doing. As much as she could not bear the thought of a life without Ewan, she did not wish to ruin his relationship with his family. "Perhaps it would be better to break off our engagement, so that your sister's family can take the time to see if they can accept it."

Ewan stepped forward and took her hands in his, then leaned down and bestowed a kiss on the back of one hand. The tender action and sensations it provoked in Ishbel were almost enough to drive all other thoughts from her head. He straightened and said, "There is nothing that you need to prove to anyone and Matilda's reaction was offensive and deplorable. It has no effect on my desire to spend my future with you. Nothing would make me happier than for you to set a date for our marriage right now."

His certainty quelled her fears. "I would rather give Lady Picton what she wants and try to win her goodwill."

"Thank you. That is generous after what you have suffered." Her squeezed her hands, his feelings for her written across his features and healing her bruised heart. "Perhaps I should arrange for a small dinner party where you can get to know my sister and her family in a relaxed setting?"

Ishbel could imagine nothing relaxed about such an event and, at the back of her mind, there was a fear that nothing she ever did would change Lady Picton's view of her, but she would try as hard as she could just the same. "Yes, that is a good idea."

They spoke for a little longer, Ewan's attitude showing that he did indeed wish for a life with her. They left the library and Ishbel's calm vanished at the sight of Harriette standing ready to pounce.

"I trust you have given your sister to understand that she has no right to ill-judge a member of my family and that the betrothal will go ahead with no further impediment," Harriette said in a glacial tone.

Ishbel said, "We remain engaged but will make no announcement of the fact until I have had more time to speak to Matilda."

Harriette's biting gaze shifted from Ishbel to Ewan. "How long exactly do you expect my cousin to dance attendance on your sister before you are willing to honour your marriage promise?"

"Harriette, stop!" Ishbel begged. "Ewan left the choice to me and I have no wish to cause unnecessary trouble between him and his family. Has Lady Picton behaved so unreasonably? If I had become engaged to a gentleman with a bad reputation would you have hesitated in speaking against it?"

She saw Harriette's ire fade a little at the truth of this argument.

"Lady Huntly," Ewan said, "I wish to appease my sister, but I promise you that my engagement and subsequent marriage to Ishbel will go ahead soon. That matters more to me than anything else."

"Very well," Harriette said. "Perhaps I should speak directly to your sister..."

"... No!" Ishbel and Ewan spoke at the same time and Harriette made the put-out expression of a cat that has had a mouse removed from its claws.

"As you wish."

29. MAKING A BAD SITUATION WORSE

"WILL YOU let me get you a drink?" Jed asked. He had ended his official work for the day so he no longer wore the blue apron that identified him as a caddie and Betsy Dale slowly looked him over and gave him a flirtatious smile, clearly thinking he was just looking to spend some money on a pretty lass. In other circumstances the dimpled grin might have turned his head, but he had other concerns right now.

"All right," she said. "I'll have a brandy."

He bought the drinks and they found a free table to sit either side of, while others played dice and cards or just talked and got drunk around them. Betsy settled the panelled skirts of her brightly coloured dress so that they wouldn't crease, her cheeks and lips reddened with rouge that enhanced her youthful features.

"I hear you knew the lassie who was murdered in an alleyway not far away." He knew Mr MacPherson and Miss Campbell had already spoken to her about her friend, but he hoped she might speak more freely to him.

Betsy pursed her lips. "Oh, is that what you're interested in?" she asked flatly.

"I'm helping to try and solve her death and there've been threats made against me and others because of it. If you liked Morag Duncan, dinna you want her killer caught?"

"Of course I do," she said, with a flash of indignation at the idea that she might feel otherwise.

"Then will you tell me what she was up to?"

"What are you talking about?" She took a gulp of her drink as if she was not planning on hanging about.

"I know she was selling stolen items, but she must have been doing more than that to cause someone to throw so much money about to it matter quiet."

"She wasna," Betsy said, brow furrowing. "She was reluctant to do that much, but George insisted that there was no harm in it. None of us thought there'd be any danger. Why should there be?"

"Did you know that she had a guinea coin on her when she was killed?"

"Aye, one of the newssheets mentioned it. She coulda sold something valuable, I s'pose."

"You canna think where else she might have got the money?"

"No." Betsy's drink sat forgotten on the table in front of her now as she fixed all her attention on him, prettier now she had stopped flirting. "I've thought about it a lot, because if it happened to her it coulda happened to any of us and I dinna want to end up dead too. All she did was maybe the occasional bit of pickpocketing and selling a few things to pawnbrokers and jewellers. It was nothing. No one would kill her for that."

She was clearly telling him all she knew and Jed reluctantly found himself agreeing with this opinion. But if Morag was not murdered over the crimes she had committed, what could she have done?

Ewan had hoped that he and Ishbel could once again begin to look forward to a bright future, that the worst problems had at least already come to light. That was until he saw the gaudily dressed visitor in his hallway.

"How dare you come and accuse my brother of murder," Nan Smith said in a loud, angry tone as soon as she saw him, before MacCuaig, the butler, could even officially announce her presence.

"I will eject this person from the house," MacCuaig responded and nodded for a footman to come forward and take one of Nan's arms.

"Get off me," she complained, trying to pull away.

This was, of course, when Picton came downstairs to find out what was going on.

"I can handle this situation," Ewan told him. "Please return to your wife."

MacCuaig had opened the front door and the footman had got Nan halfway towards it but she was determined to have her say. "George dinna kill Morag and if you tell the Town Guards otherwise..."

"... We know he is innocent," Ewan said and told the footman to let go of her since having her dragged outside would only make the situation look even worse. He could see in the periphery of his vision that Picton had not moved.

"You do?" Nan's voice lost its shrill quality. "Well, we cared about Morag so you had no right to say such things."

"I apologise for upsetting you both."

"All right then, because if I knew who'd killed her I'd tell the Town Guard or do them in myself." On this note, Nan looked with some uneasiness at all the people who were watching her and left the house of her own volition.

MacCuaig closed the door behind her and he and the footman vanished, leaving Ewan with Picton.

"What the devil was that about?" Picton demanded, making the last few steps down into the hall. "Is this the result of these odd crime enquiries of yours?"

Ewan had never wanted so much to tell a lie. "Yes."

"And is your house frequently invaded by such unwanted riffraff?"

"It has never happened before," Ewan said, "and I will endeavour to ensure that it never occurs again."

"That is not good enough," Picton said. "This business has to stop, MacPherson. You will ruin your own good name and ours as well if you continue in this way."

Ewan could have cursed the ill-timing of Nan's appearance. She could scarcely have caused more trouble for him since Picton was the one who had shown some understanding towards his feelings until now. "It was one unwanted conversation conducted in the privacy of my home. There will be no negative outcome caused to anyone by the situation."

"If you believe that, you are a fool," Picton said. "I will be removing my family from this house as soon as I possibly can."

With these words, he left, presumably to tell Matilda what had just occurred, which in turn would certainly increase her dislike of his criminal enquiries and Ishbel's part in them. Ewan did not dare believe that his standing with his family could not possibly sink any lower, just in case it somehow did.

30. MORAG'S FAMILY

TO APPEASE Harriette and also because Ishbel truly needed help, she asked Harriette's advice the next morning over breakfast on how to make a good impression on Lord and Lady Picton at the dinner party.

"You must not doubt yourself again now," Harriette told her as she buttered a slice of bread. "Any awkwardness you have ever shown in society has been due to a lack of confidence. Otherwise, you have behaved exactly as I would wish you to with the ton and you know that my standards are high."

Ishbel was touched and reassured by these words. Before she could respond, the butler held a tray out to her and she took the letter it contained and opened it. It took a moment before she could fix her mind on the murder enquiry and make sense of what she was reading. The implication changed everything. "He is alive," she said. "I must tell Ewan at once."

She stood up and Harriette said, "Is this something to do with the latest murder?"

"Yes."

"Well, you can hardly show up at Mr MacPherson's house without a chaperone or his sister will never accept you. Is he not due to call at some point today in any case?"

"He is," Ishbel said.

"Then you must exercise patience." With a noticeable lack of the virtue she had prescribed, Harriette gestured to the chair Ishbel had just vacated. "Sit down and finish your meal."

Ishbel reluctantly did so, the new information about the enquiry almost enough to put more personal worries from her mind.

When Ewan arrived at the house, she led him into the library and asked first about the intended meeting between her and Lady Picton. "Have you and your sister decided upon a date for the dinner party?"

"Yes, although there was an unforeseen snag yesterday. Nan Smith appeared at my home shouting about the injustice in our accusing her brother of Morag's murder. As a result, Picton is now set against our criminal enquiries."

"Perhaps I should finish this one alone then."

"Certainly not," he said at once. "I have as little intention of letting Picton control my life as I do of letting Matilda influence who I marry."

"If only Nan Smith had come here instead of to your home," Ishbel said. It was a blow to realise that Lord Picton was now far more likely to adopt his wife's view against Ishbel and Ewan's marriage.

Ewan smiled at her words. "Everything will resolve itself in time."

Ishbel wished she could be sure of that. "Do you wish to hear some interesting news about our current enquiry?"

"Certainly. What have you learnt?"

"I received a letter today in response to my enquiry for the information about Mrs Duncan's first husband. There was only one Marriage Certificate."

"I do not follow."

"Her marriage to Mr Duncan is the only one she has ever entered into, which means that Morag was illegitimate and her father might well still be alive."

"Then we must speak to Mrs Duncan."

"I have been considering that and I still believe we should not do so," Ishbel said. "Mr Duncan might not even be aware of this fact and it could rip apart their marriage. Besides, while I can see that it would cause embarrassment to Morag's father if she had found him, particularly if his life has the appearance of respectability, I cannot believe that her own father would kill her. We must follow this up, but it is possible that it has nothing to do with her death, in which case it would be kinder not to reveal it to Mr and Mrs Duncan."

"But how can we learn any more without speaking to Mrs

Duncan?"

"It is possible that the name of her father is on Morag's Birth Certificate."

"If the man refused to marry Mrs Duncan or was already married, he would be unlikely to let her put his name on a public document. What if you write another letter asking for this information and, if it has not been supplied, we will try to have a private conversation with Mrs Duncan?"

This idea resolved her concerns. "I will write at once."

31. FRIENDS OF THE FAMILY

"WHAT MAN do we know who took an interest in Morag's life?" Ishbel asked the next day, having given the subject some thought.

"George Smith," he said promptly from his chair in the library.

"I was meaning someone older who could be her father."

Ewan shook his head. "I can think of no one."

"What if part of the reason Morag was sent to live in another man's house when she was eleven was so her real father could get to know her without anyone suspecting the relationship?" Ishbel noticed an ink stain on the edge of one of her fingers and ineffectively tried to rub it clean.

"The family friends. Yes, that would make sense. They did offer her a home even after she committed theft, which was unusually generous."

Ishbel said, "I asked Lucy about it this morning and she only knows the general area where they lived, not the address. If we wish to visit them, we can either find out where they are from Mrs Duncan or from Lottie Miller, who we know was in touch with Morag then."

"If your theory is right, Mrs Duncan might give something away if we ask her." Seeing Ishbel's reaction, he added, "We need not mention the subject of her father but perhaps, if she is alone, she will mention him herself."

Ishbel agreed to this and they returned to the street where Morag, Lucy and Lottie had all grown up. She pictured them together, three children, whose lives would soon head in different directions – Lottie getting married, Lucy gaining a well-respected job as lady's maid and Morag, whose dishonest life somehow brought about her death.

Mrs Duncan's face paled when she opened the door to them but there was also a glint of hope in her eyes as she invited them into the parlour. Ishbel's gaze moved unintentionally to the long dining table beyond the unlit fireplace and, while she would have been buried a few days ago, in her mind's eye she could still see Morag's body laid out neatly there. Ishbel thought she had had the same mousy blonde hair as her mother but could not remember clearly and for some reason that bothered her.

Mrs Duncan made no attempt at casual conversation: there was only one thing that mattered to her. "Have you found out what happened to Morag?"

"I fear not," Ishbel said and, as if a string had been cut, Mrs Duncan's body slumped downwards in her chair. Ishbel's heart went out to her – what must it be like to lose a child? "We have in no way given up, though, and we believe her death might have a connection to the past. Could you tell us the address of the family friends Morag lived with when she was younger?"

If Mrs Duncan reacted to these words, Ishbel saw no sign of it. Ishbel wrote down the names, Mr and Mrs Adamson, and address given. There was nothing they could say to help Mrs Duncan until they could tell her why her daughter had died so they left her alone in an empty house.

Once out in the cool, foggy street, Ewan said, "Mrs Adamson might be home at this time of day but, if we want to speak to Mr Adamson, I imagine we will need to wait until an hour when he will have returned from his place of employment."

"Perhaps around five thirty this afternoon," Ishbel suggested, thinking that she would be unlikely to get back to her home before dinner was served, which would not please Harriette. Were she to arrive at the house on time but with no chance to chance her clothes, this would be viewed with equal annoyance. This all seemed inconsequential compared to the mother who had just lost her daughter.

They reached the carriage and Ewan took her hand to help her in as he agreed to collect her for the visit this evening. When they were both seated, she asked, "Have your sister and brother-in-law recovered from the turmoil of Nan Smith's visit?"

The carriage began moving at a sedate speed as he replied. "Picton has not had a civil word to say to me since then. He is out again today searching for a house to rent so as to get the family away from my bad influence as swiftly as possible."

"I am so sorry."

He smiled, although his eyes remained sad. "I fear the situation will not resolve itself any time soon but I am confident that, in time, my sister will be reconciled to my engagement to you and Picton, to the work we undertake."

"I am sure you are right," she said, although this was more hope than belief. "Perhaps the dinner party will be a step towards changing their opinions."

"Yes, it will."

It had to be, she thought, if they were ever to have a chance of an amiable relationship between them all.

"Mr Adamson isna home from his clerical job yet," Mrs Adamson said as they sat down in her parlour, with the smell of food cooking from the kitchen beyond, "but I'll be glad to answer any questions you have about Morag."

The timing of their visit had not been planned so well after all, Ishbel thought. Mrs Adamson looked at least four score years old, although her fair hair hid much of the grey. She had a long face and lines at the edges of her eyes, but her expression was good-natured.

"It must have been a shock to you to hear of her death."

"Aye, we were grief-stricken." Mrs Adamson shook her head as if she could still not quite take it in. "Morag lived with us for more than three years and we knew her all her life, so she was like family to us."

"So you continued to see her after she left your home?" Ewan asked.

"Aye, of course. She popped by every month or so, although..."

She tailed off and Ishbel prompted her, "Although?"

"I was afraid she'd given in to the temptation of un-Christian behaviour again." Mrs Adamson sighed deeply. "You know about the theft?"

"At the factory?" Ishbel checked and then agreed that they did.

"Perhaps we should have talked to her more harshly about her behaviour when that happened, but that isna the kind of people we are. I could never be stern with bairns and my husband is even more soft-hearted. Besides, her parents had obviously been angry enough – Morag could not hear the theft mentioned without her eyes filling with tears. She was ashamed of what she'd done, so we thought that would be an end of it."

"But it was not?" Ewan asked.

"I knew nothing for sure," Mrs Adamson said and moved to put another log on the fire before sitting back down, "but Morag would say so little about her life this last year. She wouldna give us her address or explain how she spent her time and there was something furtive in her manner that bothered me."

"Did she seem to have money?" Ishbel said.

"Not much, but she couldna have managed to survive if she wasna getting money from somewhere. I am almost afraid to ask, but do you know what she was up to?"

"The people she was staying with were criminals and they convinced her to sell on stolen items for them."

"How cruel of them. And that was why she died?" Mrs Adamson asked.

Before they could answer this, there were sounds from the end of the hallway and a thin man walked into the room, removing his hat before he caught sight of Ishbel and Ewan, his eyes taking in their good quality clothes. He looked to his wife questioningly.

"Arthur, these are Mr MacPherson and Miss Campbell. They are trying to find out what happened to poor Morag." He nodded and gave a polite bow to each of them before hesitating, then manoeuvring awkwardly between them to one of the remaining chairs.

"I'll check if the kettle is boiling," Mrs Adamson said and left the room.

"It is good of you to want to help Mr and Mrs Duncan," Mr Adamson said, with an accent that was not Scottish or English, although Ishbel could not place it. He had the reserved air of someone with a shy nature and looked to be a similar age to his wife. His clothes were of a sombre grey colour and he had a strongly boned face and hooked nose.

Mrs Adamson returned to say the water was still not ready and, seeing her embarrassment at not being able to provide her guests with a hot drink, Ishbel hastened to tell her that they would need to leave soon anyway as they were expected at their homes for dinner and had only called by to find out a few things.

"Were you about to say what you had found out about Morag's death?" Mrs Adamson reminded them and explained to her husband what criminal work Morag had been involved in.

"We still do not know if she died because of the stolen items she sold," Ewan said. "It may or may not be relevant to her murder but we wanted to learn more about her past. Did either of you know her father?"

Ewan looked at Mr Adamson as he spoke and Ishbel followed his gaze. Mr Adamson gave no guilty start and his expression remained sanguine. It looked as if another of their ideas was proven to be without foundation.

"No," he said. "We never knew Mrs Duncan's first husband. They began attending our church together after they were married, about two score years ago. I had seen Mr Duncan there a few times while he was single, but it was actually Morag who caused us to become friends. My wife and me have the greatest fondness for children."

He looked over at his wife, who returned his smile and took up the story, "I remember that I said to Mrs Duncan what a pretty bairn she had and after that we talked every week. When Mr Duncan found out about the factory job, we offered to let Morag stay with us as we knew her well and our own children were fully grown, two of them having left home to marry, which gave us more space. We were happy to have her here."

"Was there anything she said when you last saw her that struck you as odd or worrying?" Ishbel asked.

"There was something about her mood," Mr Adamson said and then waited for his wife to explain this.

"Yes," she said. "Morag had a nervous excitement about her, as if she had something to look forward to but wasna sure if it would be a good or bad thing."

"Did she give you any hint as to what it was?" Ewan asked, leaning forward in his chair.

"No, she dinna mention anything unusual," Mrs Adamson said, brow furrowed in thought. "She talked about her family and ours and the cold winter we were having, nothing of any importance."

"Did she talk of her father at all?"

"Her real father?" Mrs Adamson checked. "No. Why should she? She never even knew him."

They left the couple to their dinner at this point and took Ewan's carriage to her home.

"Morag mostly spoke about family," Ishbel said. "Her father might have been on her mind during the conversation, even if he was not directly spoken of."

"It was evident from Mr Adamson's behaviour that he was not Morag's father and both he and his wife seemed to have honestly cared for her. I doubt they can give us any more useful answers."

And Ishbel could think of no other middle-aged man who had been in Morag's life. Perhaps they were wrong in pursuing this idea but, although she could not have said why, Ishbel believed Morag's father mattered in some way.

32. FAMILY TROUBLES

EWAN ATE his dinner with Matilda and Picton as soon as his valet had helped him change into a more appropriate outfit. Matilda wore a satin dress for the occasion and had powdered her hair, which transformed her appearance. Ewan could not recall seeing her with whitened hair – although he must have, a few times at least – and she looked like a stranger to him. His childhood with her felt long past. Her children, she said, had been given a meal in the nursery upstairs earlier and would go to bed soon.

"I have signed the necessary papers to rent a house in Queens Street," Picton said, "so we will depart tomorrow."

"I will miss having you all here," Ewan said. The news was not unexpected but it felt as if he was losing his last chance to spend time with them. "I know we have had some disagreements since your arrival, but I do still very much want to be a part of your family's lives. I do not know if I can explain this in a way that will make sense to either of you, but the work Ishbel and I have undertaken has been for the sake of families grieving for their loved ones. The current matter we are looking into involves the murder of a young woman. I fear that the answers we find will not help Morag's parents, but at least we can give them an understanding of what events led to their daughter's death."

Matilda glanced at Picton and said, "That must be a terrible tragedy for them."

"I know you both only see the harm to my reputation in what I do," Ewan went on, "but I only see the good Ishbel and I can achieve. We try to find justice for those no one else in a position of power cares about."

"How did you learn anything of such work?" Matilda asked between raising her spoon to sip small spoonfuls of soup.

"We learned by asking questions. We try to gain enough information to piece together the dead person's life, until we can determine who killed them."

"I should have thought a woman of good birth would find such subjects too distressing and beyond her intellect," Picton commented and Ewan, who knew that his sister's education had been a thorough one, saw Matilda purse her lips.

"You forget that here in Scotland we like women to grow up strong-willed and intelligent," he said mildly. "Miss Campbell may be more academically inclined than a lot of women and certainly knows more of medical matters than I do, but there is nothing about her that I do not admire."

"Ladies in England have more feminine interests," Picton retorted, "and I am glad to say that my wife takes after them."

An image came to Ewan's mind of Matilda at around thirteen years old, running with him down a hill on their family estate, skirts flying and her face flushed red from exertion. She had won the race and he could recall the look of pride on her face at doing so.

Silence descended on the group, except for the clink of cutlery against china plates.

"I believe our mother read a great deal," Matilda said unexpectedly.

Ewan smiled at her, cheered by the implication of these words. "Yes, she did."

33. ROBERT MCLENNAN

LUCY SHOOK her head. "Robert McLennan," she repeated. "No, I never heard the name spoken by Morag's family."

"Thank you," Ishbel said and let Lucy return to her work. Morag's Birth Certificate had, against their expectations, included the name of her father, but no one they had spoken to had mentioned the man.

"Then we..." Ewan broke off as the butler walked in.

"Mr Cassell is back, miss," the butler said to Ishbel. "The mistress saw him and it did not put her in the best of moods."

Ishbel made a slight face. Harriette would get over her irritation at having a common caddie visiting the house. "Please send him in."

The butler did so. Ishbel could see why Jed's grubby apron and dirt-stained fingers would offend Harriette but to Ishbel he was someone she and Ewan could rely on and he could not be more welcome. He had a good mind too and she trusted in his abilities.

"I found out this morning that a man named Robert McLennan was Morag's father," she said. "He was not, as we had previously thought, ever married to Mrs Duncan. Perhaps he was already married when she met him or maybe he refused to marry her, even after she found out she would bear his child. Have you heard the name mentioned by anyone?"

"No, Miss Campbell," Mr Cassell said. "I can ask around, but it's not an uncommon name."

"There would have been a connection between him and Mrs Duncan. Her maiden name was..." Ewan frowned and looked at

Ishbel.

"Elizabeth Grey," she supplied.

"Yes, miss," Miss Cassell said. "I've kept asking about Morag and none of the local shopkeepers remember seeing her on the day she died. It could be that someone dishonest dinna want us to know he had illegal dealings with her or that she was doing something other than shopping."

Ishbel thought about the alley where Morag had died. It was close to the centre of the city, with streets of shops at either end of it and the law courts nearby. "We know she had criminal acquaintances, so perhaps she was watching a trial."

"I can find out what cases were in the courts that day," Mr Cassell said at once. "There are also flats above many of the shops. She might have visited someone's home. If any trial or building brings up a familiar name, I'll let you know."

He left them to continue their discussion alone and Ishbel rang for coffee and refreshments to be served.

"I think Matilda might be thawing slightly," Ewan said and told her about the dinner conversation with his family the previous evening.

Ishbel was happy to hear what he said, hoping it meant that Matilda would give her a chance to talk frankly when they saw each other at the dinner party which would take place the next evening. "What sorts of books did your mother like?"

"She liked to find out about plants," Ewan said, "and she read novels sometimes, although I remember my father would make disparaging comments about the latter. He felt that they gave women fanciful ideas."

"That depends on the novels," Ishbel said. "Harriette often reads them and I doubt anyone would dare accuse her of having got any foolish notions from a book."

"No," he agreed with feeling and she smiled. He continued, "I am certain that my mother would have thought well of you. Most of my memory is of her being ill and I was still quite a young child when she died, but she had a way of quickly understanding people's hearts. I wish you could have met her."

"So do I," Ishbel said, glad to know more of his past.

34. AWKWARD CONVERSATIONS

ISHBEL WAS relieved to be greeted in a civil way by Lady Picton when she arrived at the dinner party. There was an awkwardness between them, which was to be expected after what had happened when they last saw each other, but Ishbel thought that perhaps Lady Picton wanted to give her a chance and get to know her now. Harriette, of course, then gave Lord and Lady Picton the iciest of greetings which effectively cut short any exchange of pleasantries for the moment.

As Ewan and his family welcomed the next arrivals, Ishbel crossed the drawing room to speak to Miss Chiverton, who looked up with a dimpled smile and left her brother and Mr McDonald's side to join her. The women curtsied and Miss Chiverton indicated the two men and said, "They are discussing upcoming fashions. How is it that men can discuss their tailors and horses for hours, yet they accuse women of having no intellectual ability?"

"I cannot believe your brother would say such a thing," Ishbel said as they meandered towards the refreshments table.

"Eddie would not but Henry, like our father, enjoys a belief that women are an inferior species. And Mr McDonald is endlessly condescending towards me — is it not peculiar that two interesting gentlemen like Mr MacPherson and my brother would pick someone so dull to befriend?"

"I am not well acquainted with Mr McDonald," Ishbel said, surprised as this assessment, "but he has shown kindness to me when I needed it and I assume that he would not still choose to be friends with people who both, to an extent, flout society's conventions unless he had sides to his personality that are perhaps not readily apparent."

"Please excuse me," Miss Chiverton said at once. "I do not normally slander those around me and Mr McDonald is not always objectionable, but since I came out into society he has felt he has some right as a family acquaintance to give me advice on propriety. I have just now received a ten-minute lecture from him about the colour of dress an unmarried lady should wear."

"I can see how that would be irritating." Ishbel took in the pale-yellow gown Miss Chiverton was wearing tonight. "Even if it were any man's right to comment on such matters, I can see nothing he could object to in your current outfit."

"Nor did he, or I would have scolded him fiercely," Miss Chiverton said with spirit and Ishbel burst out laughing. The two women giggled for several minutes, which made Ishbel realise how much she had needed some levity after the difficulties from the last week. From Miss Chiverton's reaction she too had been under a strain lately and Ishbel recalled what she had said when they last saw each other about unwanted suitors.

They reached their destination and a footman handed them the drinks they asked for, Ishbel taking a ratafia while Miss Chiverton claimed a glass of lemonade. They turned back towards the other guests but did not hurry to end their private conversation. Ewan and Lord and Lady Picton were still conversing with new arrivals so Ishbel could not yet approach them.

"Have you had any more marriage proposals?" she asked.

"Two," Miss Chiverton said, "and Mama had a stern word with me about making up my mind who to marry. Is there something wrong with me that I do not feel ready to be a wife?"

"Not in the least and a marriage to the wrong person must be intolerable." She thought of her own parents' unhappiness and compared it with the strength of her love for Ewan. She would hate to see a friend trapped in a bad marriage.

"There is no man I even strongly like, let alone love."

"Then you must find a way to convince your parents to allow you to wait. Many young women take a couple of seasons in society before they wed and you have only been out a matter of months. Perhaps your brother could speak to them on your behalf?"

"That would not help in the slightest. Now that Eddie is independent and spending almost all his time with Alex... You do know..?" Miss Chiverton broke off and bit her lip.

Ishbel knew at once what she was being asked. She remembered her initial astonishment at learning that Mr Chiverton was romantically involved with another man, but her shock had quickly faded and she thought now that perhaps his unconventional choices were not so different to hers. They both wished to live in such a way as made them happy. "I know," she told Miss Chiverton. "I have a high opinion of your brother and, while I have only met Alex a few times, I have always found him a pleasant man."

"He is like another brother to me, one as amenable as Eddie. I think Mama could perhaps accept him, although she has never directly said so, but Papa rules our family and he and Henry could scarcely be more opposed to the relationship. They do not try to understand Eddie's feelings and now they are insisting that I only spend time with him at public events."

"That must be difficult for you both." It made Ishbel realise how much freedom she had in her own life. Harriette had not always been so accepting but Ishbel had refused to give up the things that made her happy, namely the academic work and criminal enquiries, and Harriette had slowly come to terms with it.

"I do not intend to waste this afternoon feeling despondent, so pray tell me all that has happened with the murder you and Mr MacPherson are looking into."

Ishbel told her what they had learnt of Morag's father and how Jed Cassell was helping them find out more about Morag's involvement in crime.

Miss Chiverton listened to this intently before saying, "So the dead woman could either having been meeting others involved in crimes on the day she died, which led to her death, or she might have had an innocent errand and died for another reason?"

"Exactly. It seems likely that her illegal work had something to do with her murder but there may have been some other cause we have not even discovered yet."

"How interesting to put all the threads together, like a piece of embroidery, and gradually see a picture appearing which solves everything."

Ishbel looked round the room and saw that all the guests had now arrived. She caught Ewan's eye and he gave a slight nod.

Miss Chiverton saw the exchange and said, "Shall we join Mr MacPherson's family?"

"If you do not mind. I need to find a way to win his sister's approval."

"Yes, of course," Miss Chiverton agreed. "I am sure that as soon as she spends a little time with you, she cannot help but like you."

Ishbel smiled gratefully and they walked arm-in-arm over to the group that consisted of Mr MacPherson, Lord and Lady Picton, Lady Morrelly and Mr and Mrs Hellerton, a couple advanced in their years Ishbel had been introduced to but barely knew. Her nerves grew as they drew closer but Ewan's aunt turned and gave her a friendly smile.

"How lovely you look this evening, Miss Campbell," she said.

"As do you."

"Nonsense." Lady Morrelly made a dismissive gesture. "I care little about my appearance these days. If my maid has managed to remove the cat hairs from my dress, I am content."

They all smiled at this and Ishbel found the courage to turn to Lady Picton. "How are you enjoying being back in your home city, my lady?"

Ewan's sister responded politely, "Very much, Miss Campbell, although it has changed greatly and is continuing to do so with the creation of the New Town."

"I believe it will be elegant when it is completed."

"Lord Picton and I have just moved into a house in Queens Street so all the new amenities are an easy distance from us."

"MacPherson," Mr Monro said, joining them. He worked at the University so Lord Huntly had introduced them and Ishbel had spoken to him at a few formal events. "What is this I hear about you dragging Miss Campbell into another wretched murder business? Have you not had enough of causing scandals?"

Mr Monro's tone was a friendly one so he clearly meant the words to be taken in a jovial manner, but there was a pause where no one moved or spoke and the atmosphere was thick with tension. Ishbel saw the frown that formed on both Lord and Lady Picton's features and she winced internally. She forced herself to take a sip of her drink as if nothing was amiss, while she searched her mind for something innocuous to say.

"There are no scandals involved," Ewan responded, his calm tone a little forced. "That is the last thing we would want. A young woman died in strange circumstances and we have agreed to help her friends and family find out why; that is all."

"Yes, of course." Mr Monro said, seeming to realise, as his eyes darted round the assembled group, that his comment had caused a problem. "It was a poor choice of words. I would certainly not find fault with anyone who is making the most of their brains as you and Miss Campbell are doing. What is the point of a good education if it is not utilised?"

Ewan's strained expression eased. "I find my education is continuing every day as I try to understand what motivates people to act the way they do."

"Ah, there has in fact been some interesting academic work done recently on that subject. I will see if I can borrow the latest reports to pass on to you, or to Miss Campbell if I see her first at the college."

"I am sure we would both appreciate that," Ewan said as Harriette and Lord Huntly joined them. Harriette's husband also worked at Edinburgh University so he was happy to enter into the conversation and keep it on such academic subjects.

Ishbel glanced round to see how Lord and Lady Picton were reacting to the topic and caught the eye of Ewan's sister, who said, "Ewan told me that you read about medicine and other subjects but I was not aware that you spent any time at the university." She did not sound pleased to hear it now.

"Yes," Ishbel said, since there would be no point in denying the fact. She had always taken pride in the work so why did she now feel as though she were admitting to a crime? "I attend a number of lectures there every week."

Lord Picton's eyebrows shot upwards and he viewed her with horror. "Do you mean that you are spoken to by male professors in a public setting about such vulgar topics as the appearance of the male body?"

"I have always been treated there with the utmost respect." Ishbel refrained from saying that she had watched a number of autopsies of male corpses or Ewan's family would never speak to her again. "I like to learn, as does everyone who attends the college."

"Quite so," said Lord Huntly with a fond smile at her. "It would be a tragedy for someone as bright as Ishbel to be denied such an opportunity."

Harriette did not look as if she entirely endorsed her husband's view but said to Lord and Lady Picton, "Ishbel's father worked at the university so she has spent time there from the time she was old enough to walk and the other professors still speak of the late Mr Campbell with admiration, so they would never allow any harm to befall his daughter."

"I see." Lady Picton's tone was unemotional and Ishbel did not think her cousin's words had been enough to change Lord and Lady Picton's minds.

Someone walking behind Ishbel and accidentally nudged her, and Ishbel started. Some of contents of her glass splashed over her hand and onto the edge of Lady Picton's dress, leaving a collection of damp drops on the green silk. Lady Picton breathed in sharply as she – and everyone else – took in the mark.

"Forgive me," Ishbel said, her cheeks flaming. "Let me get a napkin to clean the stain."

"A maid will do that," Lady Picton said curtly with a frown, as if Ishbel's response, like everything else about her, was at fault.

The woman turned away without another word and left the room. Ishbel watched her go with a clenching feeling in her chest as she took in the fact that she might have just ruined her one opportunity to obtain Lady Picton's goodwill and a blessing for Ishbel's engagement to Ewan.

35. A DEAD END

"YOUR CLUMSINESS was not well timed, but I am sure Lady Picton will not condemn you forever for it." Harriette's attempt to comfort her the next morning only added to Ishbel's mortification at what she had done. They were alone, sitting at either end of the long dining table breaking their fasts, Lord Huntly having already eaten and left for the university.

Ishbel had spent a restless night lying awake, miserable at the thought that she might be losing Ewan. This situation was even more difficult for him than her as he was caught between the love he felt for his sister and his affection for Ishbel. "I do not believe there is anything I can say or do to make her like me now."

"Nonsense." Harriette took a sip of chocolate from a dainty china cup. "You must simply try harder. Would you give up on an academic issue so easily?"

Ishbel groaned at the unintentional reminder of another concern. "I believe she holds my academic work against me too."

"I have never been thrilled that you go off to university lectures, but it does not stop me caring for you."

"You are my family."

"You can be certain that that fact would never control my emotions nor prevent me from speaking my mind."

Ishbel was certain and felt a little better.

The butler entered the room and said in a tone of the greatest reluctance. "Mr Cassell is here to see Miss Ishbel, my lady."

"Is that man now permanently employed by you and Mr

MacPherson?" Harriette snapped.

Ishbel smiled as she stood up. "I am relieved to know that your irritation over what I do with my life will not affect our affectionate relationship."

Harriette merely rolled her eyes and Ishbel walked into the hallway where Jed Cassell stood in his work clothes, his shoulders slightly hunched as if he was waiting for someone to tell him he was not allowed to be inside such a fine house. He could not be more than sixteen years of age and she wondered how young he had been when he first began his job as a caddie. This murder was showing her how difficult the lives of working-class children could be.

"Mr Cassell, please come into the drawing room," Ishbel said, smiling at him. "Would you like some coffee?"

"No thank you, Miss Campbell." His shoulders straightened as he followed her into the spacious room where they both sat down, facing each other. He had surrendered his hat to the butler and, without that to hold, he seemed unsure what to do with his hands, placing them on the arms of his carved chair, before changing his mind and moving them to rest on his lap. She was familiar with the feeling of not knowing how to act around people in certain situations and spoke gently to him.

"What have you discovered about Morag's father, Robert McLennan?"

"Nothing, I'm afraid." He looked unhappy at having to admit this. "There are a few men with that name in Edinburgh but none seems to have any connection to Mrs Duncan and none are known to be criminals."

"Then it is likely that her father is dead," Ishbel said.

"That or he left the city a long time ago."

Either way, he could not have been involved in Morag's murder, which was disappointing. She had been sure he was relevant to the murder in some way. "We seem to be having great trouble moving forward with this matter."

"I dinna have any luck finding where Morag was before she died either. There was no one living in the area where she died who seemed to be known to her. There were several trials at the courts that day but, again, there dinna seem to be any connection between the criminals and her. Mebbe she was just cutting through the alley on her way to somewhere further away."

"Or someone does not wish us to know that they met with her."

"Perhaps," he agreed.

"And no one saw anyone with blood on their clothes on the day she died?"

"No, miss, and there might be money in information like that so, if they'd seen such a person, someone would say." He frowned and was silent for a moment before saying, "It dinna make sense, does it? He couldna have killed her in such a messy way without getting some blood on him and, if he wasna seen, he must live near there. I'll keep asking questions."

She thanked him but, as he left, she could think of little more she and Ewan could do without further information. Most of the people they had spoken to had little knowledge of what Morag's life had been like for the last year and George and Nan Smith were hardly likely to tell them anything else.

She hated to consider the possibility but perhaps this murder was destined to remain unsolved.

36. MISS CHIVERTON TRIES TO HELP

MISS CHIVERTON stepped down from her carriage, looked up at the assembly rooms and smiled. She had learned the steps to every modern dance and liked having the opportunity to show what she had been taught at a ball.

Her father and mother walked sedately towards the open door, her hand on his arm, followed by her brother and his fiancée. Mr McDonald, who had somehow ended up joining them, held out his arm to her and she took it, eager to be inside. She hoped some of her friends would be here... and that there none of her would-be suitors would attend.

"Your dress is most becoming," Mr McDonald said as they reached the door and walked into the building, to be immediately surrounded by people.

"Thank you," she responded carelessly, searching the room for a familiar face.

"An unmarried lady can never go wrong with a white gown."

She pursed her lips and did not dignify this with an answer.

"May I fetch you a drink?"

"Yes, that would be pleasant." She gave a sigh of relief as he walked away and stood on the periphery of her family's group, letting the conversation they were having with older friends wash over her as she continued to look round the room. It was full of groups of talking people, the men and married women dressed in bright colours like peacocks, while the unmarried women were more like pale lambs trotting along at their mother's sides.

She caught a glimpse of a familiar face and moved to her father's side. "Papa, there is Mr MacPherson with his sister and brother-in-law. Since you and Mama have not yet met them, will you not allow Henry to introduce you to them? Mr MacPherson is, after all, very good friends with Eddie." She saw a frown wrinkle his brow at the mention of her other brother and hastily amended her words. "I believe you would find Lord and Lady Picton to be agreeable, refined people."

"Very well," her father said and they approached the group. Mr MacPherson was as charming as ever and dressed in an emerald coat with gold buttons that made him the most handsome gentleman in the room. Fiona thought, a touch wistfully, that Miss Campbell was lucky.

Introductions were being made as Mr McDonald returned and handed her a drink. She thanked him and hastily took a large sip, wary of accidents after what had happened at the dinner party. Mr McDonald and Mr MacPherson exchanged nods and Mr McDonald complimented Lady Picton on her gown, since he was apparently determined to speak of nothing but clothing tonight.

"Is Miss Campbell here?" Fiona asked Mr MacPherson and ignored the unhappy expressions of some of the group.

"I believe not," he said.

"I do hope you will not hold her clumsiness against her, Lady Picton. It is most unlike her and was due, I am sure, to nerves. Miss Campbell is the most agreeable lady of my acquaintance, always sensible and good-natured."

"I am glad to hear it," Lady Picton said with an unreadable glance at her husband.

As the subject of the conversation changed to more mundane topics, Fiona wished she could have spoken better on behalf of her friend. She was not sure her words had done any good at all.

The two groups drifted apart to speak to different people, her parents joining a larger group and when her brother asked his fiancée to dance, Fiona was left alone with Mr McDonald, which was not at all what she wanted.

"What do you think, Lord Tain?"

The voice nearby made her turn her head. How did she know that name? Then, with excitement, she recalled Miss Campbell's murder enquiry.

"Do you know Lord Tain?" she asked Mr McDonald.

"A little."

"Would you introduce me?"

"Why?" he asked.

"Because he is said to be an interesting, learned gentleman," she lied.

Mr McDonald's expression was perplexed. "You should not try to copy Miss Campbell too much." Fiona's heart sunk at the thought that her true reason had been discerned by him. He continued, "While I like and admire the lady, her academic leanings are not entirely approved of by society."

Fiona brightened as she realised he had not guessed her true purpose. "Surely a young lady would not be criticised for listening to an intelligent man talk? In my limited experience, it is what many gentlemen most enjoy."

He narrowed his eyes at the hint of impertinence in this remark but just said, "Very well."

They approached the small group and he introduced her to Lord and Lady Tain and their companions, Mr and Mrs Fraser. Lord Tain was a middle-aged man, his hair hidden beneath a powdered wig, the rose red in his white-and-red striped coat matching the red in his wife's dress. Lady Tain was perhaps ten years younger than him and held his arm in a proprietary way. Mr Fraser, a short gentleman with a sallow complexion, was a newly qualified solicitor who seemed to have an endless list of legal questions he wished to ask of the older man.

"I fear this conversation will be dull for you," Lady Tain said to Fiona in a slightly condescending way. She was the only one of the group they had joined who spoke in the upper class English accent rather than a Scottish one.

"Not at all. I imagine the legal profession must be a fascinating one."

"It is a distinguished career my husband excels at."

"I should think it would be a thrilling thing to watch him present a case in front of the judge and jury."

"It makes me very proud."

Lord Tain overheard this remark and gave his wife an affectionate smile, patting the gloved hand that rested on his arm.

Fiona said to him, "My friend, Miss Campbell, told me recently about your kindness to Morag Duncan, a child accused of theft."

"Aye, I recall Mr MacPherson and Miss Campbell having an interest in the girl. Tell me, have they worked out what happened to her?"

"Not yet."

"What is this?" Lady Tain asked.

Her husband said, "It is a tragic matter. The working-class girl, Morag Duncan, was my client when, as a child, she committed a theft. I managed to convince the factory woman she stole from not to bring the matter to trial and sincerely hoped Miss Duncan would do better in the future. Her recent death was in the newssheets – she was murdered in the ugliest way."

"How can that possibly matter to anyone here?" Lady Tain said in a dismissive way that shocked Fiona. "Women of that class die every day. I do not see why you should give it any thought."

Lord Tain frowned, looking taken aback. "It is my job to do so."

"Surely your work is to defend people to the best of your ability. The mistakes they make after you help them cannot be on your conscience – that is all I meant."

"That is true," he said and the conversation resumed with a discussion between Mr Fraser and Lord Tain on a recent trial involving a small gang of thieves who, Lord Tain believed, still had accomplices at large in society.

Although the subject was interesting, Fiona only half listened. She had hoped to find out something to help Miss Campbell and Mr MacPherson but had learnt nothing, except that Lady Tain had a callous streak and now Mr McDonald, who had finally worked out what she was up to, was glaring at her.

She ignored him and wondered if she could find someone to dance with.

37. JED FACES DANGER

JED BACKED away from the three men, only realising too late that they had manoeuvred him into a coal yard, with no way of escape. It was early morning and his mind had still been on the bills for his brother's medicine and treatment. Despite knowing that someone did not want Morag Duncan's murder solved, Jed had not been careful enough and, seeing the threat he faced, he realised he might not get another chance.

"You shoulda listened to all the warnings, boy," one of the men said, echoing Jed's thoughts. The speaker was a fair-haired thug of around thirty with a long scar on one muscular arm, and, as nervous as he was, Jed bristled at being referred to as a child. He was just as brawny as the man he faced and was confident he could have got the best of him in a fight. But not of all of them together. Gabe Fryer, the criminal who'd warned him off before, was with them and Jed had an idea that he recognised another of the men as having spent time in gaol too. They were a rough-looking collection and Jed had the feeling they were not here to just beat him up.

"Your patrons, Miss Campbell and Mr MacPherson, shoulda dropped the matter after I spoke to you before," Gabe said. "With the reward money promised, I'll gladly risk hanging for all of you. If others dinna get to them first, that is. Even if they do, the money on your head is definitely ours."

"Aye," the blond agreed and picked up a shovel that had been lying next to a heap of coal, holding it up as a weapon.

The three of them spread out as they approached Jed, so they could attack him together. He had to think of some way to distract them or he would not stand a chance. He backed further away, feeling behind him with his feet for stacks of coal, as tripping over now would be fatal.

"If you're gonna kill me anyway, why not tell me who it is that's paying for me to die?"

The blond laughed with genuine amusement, the sound rattling Jed. "I dinna ken who's offered the reward but whoever it is has deep pockets."

Jed tried to keep an eye on all three of the man as they surrounded him, tensed for the beginning of an attack. "So how do you know they'll really pay?"

"Their hired man was open-handed with me just for giving you the warning you stupidly ignored," Gabe said and made a lunge at Jed, who blocked the punch and shoved him away, getting to one side of the thugs. There was still a man standing in his way but, if he could get around him, Jed could get out of here and make a run for it.

"Why take the chance of hanging when you can make a good profit from selling this information to Mr MacPherson?" Jed suggested and saw one of them pause to consider the idea.

"Because he's already as good as dead and if we dinna kill you, someone else'll do it and claim the reward," Gabe said and sprang forward, the speed of the attack too fast for Jed to counter, and he was knocked to the ground.

Gabe punched Jed, the blow making his senses spin, but desperation kept his wits sharp and he grabbed Gabe's wrist with one hand and clenched the other into a fist to return the blow, landing it in Gabe's stomach. Jed rolled away just as the second man brought the shovel down with crushing force on the spot where his head had been.

Jed tried to jump to his feet but the blond grabbed his ankle, sending him sprawling again. Panic set in as the three of them descended on him at once. Heart thumping as he saw his own death in their eyes, Jed aimed a punch at the man with the shovel before the red-head who'd previously hung back punched him in the face.

"Oy! What are you doing?"

The unknown voice was the most welcome sound Jed could imagine. As the assault was paused, he caught sight of a couple of men entering the yard from the street. Their faces and arms were covered in black coal dust, so they obviously worked here.

There was a pause and then Gabe Fryer made a run for it while the other thugs dithered, still crouched over Jed.

"Langham, go fetch the Town Guard who's out on the street," the older coal worker said and the younger man raced off.

One of the men who held Jed, a fist around his neck, swore and let go, and both of them hurriedly got up and jogged for the main street.

The coal worker took in Jed's blue apron with a frown. "How badly are you hurt, laddie?"

"I'm fine, thanks to you," Jed answered, sitting up. His face was tender but his nose was not broken and he had no other injury, to his surprise. Having feared being killed, he could not quite take in his fortune. The man reached out a large hand and hauled Jed to his feet.

"What was all that about?"

"Someone put out a reward to kill me." He breathed in sharply as he remembered what the thugs had said. "I have to go – two others are in danger too."

At that moment, of course, the Town Guard appeared, with the lad who had been sent to get him and demanded a full account. Jed answered the questions as quickly as he could, desperate to warn Mr MacPherson and Miss Campbell.

He could only hope he would not reach them too late.

38. SUDDEN VIOLENCE

"I FEAR we have discovered nothing that has any direct bearing on Morag's death," Ewan said, sitting in a more relaxed pose than usual in his seat beside the library fire. He put a hand over his mouth to hide a yawn and straightened. "Forgive me – I stayed late at a ball last night, one where young Miss Chiverton sang your praises to my sister and Picton."

"How kind of her," Ishbel said with feeling, glad to have become friends with the younger woman. "Do you think it helped make up for my blunders at your home?"

"Do you mean, getting a few drops of your drink on Matilda's dress? That was nothing – it did not leave the smallest stain. I hope you have not been worrying about something so trivial."

His reaction was heartening, convincing her that perhaps Lady Picton would not hold it against her after all. "I do not think your family was impressed to hear about me attending lectures either."

"That is not their concern. It is unusual but nothing they can find fault with."

She was not convinced about that and adding it to the work she did on murder enquiries, Ishbel was hardly the sort of young lady his sister might want him to marry.

"Since the weather has been fine the last few days, I thought we might carry out McDonald's suggestion of a picnic. That would let my sister get to know you properly in a relaxed setting."

"That is a charming plan." She resolved not to drink anything during the event or Lady Picton would be afraid to come near her.

"Three days from today?"

That would be a Saturday, when there were no lectures for her to attend at the university, although she would have cancelled any other plans for the sake of another chance to attempt to make a good impression on Ewan's family. She was determined to succeed this time. "That is perfect."

"I will have my butler make the arrangements."

There was a silence and then Ishbel returned to their original subject. "I fear the subject of Morag's father is a pointless one. He is most likely dead and, even if Morag had discovered a relation of his, why would they possibly harm her?"

"Yes. I think you are right. That takes us back to the crimes she was involved in."

"So who could have given Morag the guinea and why? George Smith seemed to know nothing about it."

"No and it was certainly not obtained honestly."

She tapped her finger on the leather cover of a book. "It must have been one of the people she sold stolen items to – nothing else makes sense. We just have to find a way to convince them to talk to us."

"If money is what most matters to them, perhaps we could use it to encourage them to speak."

"Yes." She stood up. "Let us try that."

A short time later Ewan's carriage stopped in front of one of the shops they had visited before. They walked inside and were approached, more warily than the first time they had visited, by the snub-nosed middle-aged proprietor.

They abandoned the pretence they had previously used of being innocent shoppers and Ewan opened his money pouch, removing several coins. "We have no interest in causing trouble over any illegal behaviour we discover," he said, holding them out to the man, who looked nervously around, before pocketing them. "We just wish to know about Morag Duncan. You know who that is?"

"Aye," the man said in a low tone. He looked them over at length, as if deciding whether or not to trust them and then he gestured for them to follow him into the back part of the shop, which was a small office. Once they were alone, he spoke more freely. "Morag started coming here eight or nine months ago, bringing items for me to sell. I dinna ask where they came from – I canna afford to be fussy."

"Was she here on the day she died?" Ishbel asked.

"No, I hadna seen her in a few days when I heard of her death."

Then this trip was another futile one. Where had Morag been before she was killed?

"Do you know of anyone who wanted to harm her?"

"I asked around quietly after she died. After all, someone coming after her might have also been after me, but no one knew anything. I thought she must have stolen something from the wrong person."

"No, it was George Smith who did the stealing," Ewan said.

"Who told you that?" the man scoffed. "That young man wouldna risk his own neck if he could get someone else to risk theirs."

"Then perhaps the money Morag had on her came directly from a theft," Ishbel said to Ewan.

"Or she sold on something too valuable and the owner had her killed over it," the shop owner suggested. "But it's nothing I've heard about."

Ishbel was lost in thought as they left the shop, going from the darkness of the back room through the dim shop and out into the overcast street. She had no idea where the attackers came from. One moment, she was walking towards the carriage with Ewan at her side and the next, one muscular man had got hold of Ewan while another knocked her off her feet.

She shrieked as she saw the first man produce a knife. Ewan punched him and, as she hurriedly got to her feet, she saw the knife flash towards him. She could not breathe as she heard Ewan's grunt of pain and saw him stagger back several steps, the sleeve of his jacket covered in a growing stain of blood.

She stared at the knife, held in a confident grip, terrified that the man would use it again and kill Ewan. Instead, the men paused less than an arm's length away from her and one of them pointed a finger at Ewan and then turned towards her. "You shoulda left Morag Duncan's murder alone. Now it's too late for you."

Ishbel froze as their hard gazes fell on her, like wolves spying their prey. Ewan moved unsteadily to stand in front of her and raised his fists. Although he was tall, he was also slender and faced men whose arms bulged with muscles and whom she saw both carried knives. One of them looked happy to meet the challenge and Ishbel looked around for something to throw at him, but the other pulled him back. They caught sight of something that made them pause before running off and, sick with relief, Ishbel realised what it was when Ewan's carriage driver raced to her side, the little tiger beside him taking Ewan's uninjured arm.

"Do you want me to go after that ruffian, sir?" the carriage driver asked. Although he was smartly dressed, he was a sturdy-looking man, whose look of anger at the attack on his master suggested he was keen to pursue them.

"No," Ewan said. "I do not want you to risk your life over this."

They all looked round at the attackers, just as the men reached the end of the street and turned out of view.

39. RESOLUTIONS

"IF SOMEONE is afraid of what we will find out, at least it shows we are progressing in the right direction," Ewan said in a calm tone while Ishbel bit her lip as she watched the elderly physician apply ointment to the gash on his arm, reminded of a similar occasion when he had been wounded during their pursuit of a killer. He might have died today. She could have lost him.

"This is lunacy," Harriette said, hands on hips as she watched the proceedings that were taking place in her drawing room. "You cannot possibly pursue this matter further if it puts your lives in danger."

"On the contrary," Ishbel said, trying to sound composed. Faced with Ewan's injury, she wanted to say the opposite words to the ones she knew she had to speak. "It would be insupportable to give in to such bullying tactics."

"I agree," Ewan said at once, as the physician stoppered the ointment bottle and then began to bandage his arm.

"No, this is my doing," came a voice from the doorway and they all turned their heads to see Lucy standing in the doorway, an appalled expression on her face. "I should never have got you involved in this matter, miss. You have to stop."

Harriette gestured to the maid. "There. Now there is no need for you to continue with this folly."

"There is a young woman whose murderer is still at large," Ewan said from his chair.

"Harriette, were an important member of society to snub you, you would never allow the slight to pass unchallenged," Ishbel said.

"It is hardly a good comparison. There would be no risk to my life in that situation." Harriette was finishing speaking when a new figure appeared, walking past Lucy towards Ewan and Ishbel. Jed Cassell bowed to Harriette and the others, but she ignored him and said to Ishbel, "You and I will discuss this later in private."

Harriette glared at Jed as she passed him and swept out of the room, skirts rustling. Ishbel got a clearer look at Jed's face as he moved closer and breathed in sharply as she saw bruises darkening it.

"I'm sorry," Jed said to Ishbel and Ewan, "I had three thugs attack me earlier. They said there was a reward for killing all of us, but I couldna get here in time to warn you. The reward is there for anyone to claim, so we're all in danger until the murder is solved."

Ewan leaned forward. "How bad are your injuries?"

"Just what you can see, sir. By good luck alone, I came out of my fight better than you did."

"I think we were all lucky," Ishbel said, "and it sounds as if it is too late for us to stop our enquiries now, even if we were to decide that we wished to."

"Aye," Jed agreed unhappily.

Ewan reached into his money pouch and took out a number of coins. He stood and walked across the room to put them into Jed's hand. "Take this and find somewhere to stay out of sight until we get the matter solved. I do not want your death on my conscience."

Jed stared in shock at the coins. "This is a fortune."

"You have more than earned it," Ewan told him. "You were hurt because of us."

"No," Jed contradicted him, "I was hurt by the killer's order. I chose to accept your hire, so I was always willing to accept the chance of danger. And if you intend to keep on with the hunt, then I will too. If it helps you any, the thugs let slip that they dinna know who'd offered the reward as it was offered through a go-between, but given the money involved the murderer would have to either be a powerful criminal or an aristocrat."

"That information will certainly help," Ewan said.

Jed pocketed the money and took his leave of them, so only Lucy remained. Ishbel hoped Mr Cassell would be careful. The recent violence had left her feeling ill and unnerved.

"It's not right for you to be at risk over something I asked you to do," Lucy said. She was still standing close to the door, her hands clasped so tightly that the knuckles were white.

"It is also wrong for Morag to have been killed," Ishbel said, getting to her feet. "We cannot allow her murderer to remain free, but I promise that we will be as careful as we possibly can."

Lucy did not look much reassured by this promise but, used to obeying Ishbel, she nodded and returned to her work, a frown creasing her brow as she departed. She could not possibly have known there would be any danger when she had asked Ishbel to find out about her friend and Ishbel would reassure her further later, not wanting her to worry.

Alone with Ewan, Ishbel ventured to touch his hand, her ungloved fingers resting briefly on the warm skin. "I hate to see you hurt."

He took her hand and bent at the waist to kiss it, which sent a tingling sensation through her whole body. "We will both need to keep servants nearby to put off any further attacks until this matter is resolved."

"I will do so," she promised, sufficiently concerned by what had happened that she would be glad to know they both had protection. Then, thinking of all they had gone through today, she silently pledged that the murderer who had thought to silence them would soon be made to regret his misdeeds.

40. THE PICNIC

THE WEATHER proved astonishingly cooperative on the day of the picnic, the sun shining down from a deep blue sky. Ewan already had Lord and Lady Picton in his carriage, along with their three children and a governess, when he called to collect Ishbel, the rest of the party taking a second carriage to meet them at the agreed location. Harriette and Lord Huntly had a prior engagement which Ishbel thought might be for the best, since Harriette's blunt comments were not to everyone's taste. It was difficult for her to relax and enjoy the outing after the recent threats to their lives, but Ishbel's desire to improve her relationship with Lady Picton was just as strong as her fear. She wanted there to be no reason for Lady Picton to possibly take offence at today.

Apparently it was already too late.

Ishbel took her seat beside Ewan and opposite his sister. "I hope your arm is not too sore," she said quietly to him, the thought of the deep cut hidden by both bandage and coat making her heart lurch.

"It barely hurts."

"That seems to be down to luck alone," Lady Picton said icily. "I find it extraordinary that so many people have told me how intelligent you both are, when neither of you has the sense to stay away from such dangerous situations."

"We were outside a shop in the middle of the city," Ewan said mildly. "There could have been no reason to fear for our safety."

"Is that also your opinion, Miss Campbell?" Lady Picton's eyes were hard.

She hesitated. "There is an element of peril in the work we do. As much as we wish it were not so, we are both willing to take that risk because we believe in the importance of what we are doing."

"You feel no shame in making your family worry for your safety?"

"I could be killed tomorrow by a runaway carriage or next week by an unexpected illness. Ewan – Mr MacPherson and I do all we can to avoid coming to harm, but not every danger is foreseeable."

"It is more dignified and certainly safer for a lady to remain at home, taken care of by her family," Lord Picton said.

Ishbel glanced over at the children: the baby was asleep in the arms of the governess while the older children pointed out animals they could see from the carriage window. She said quietly, "Your wife risked her life three times to give birth to your lovely children. Would either one of you ever wish she had not been so brave?"

Lord Picton looked taken aback by this and neither he nor his wife answered. Silence fell for much of the journey, Ewan and Ishbel's attempts at making conversation met with terse answers. Ishbel could not blame Lady Picton for being troubled over Ewan's injury but could think of nothing to say that would in any way reassure her. The idea of him being in danger scared her too but he would make his own decision on what he was willing to take risks for, just as Ishbel did.

They were a subdued group when they met up with the rest of their party in a patch of countryside that looked down on a good-sized loch, so the smiling faces of Mr Chiverton, Miss Chiverton and Mr McDonald were a welcome sight.

As greetings were exchanged, Miss Chiverton whispered to Ishbel, "I met Lord and Lady Tain at a ball recently. I did not learn much but I will tell you about it when we have a little privacy."

"I look forward to hearing about it," Ishbel responded in a similarly hushed tone and, as they turned to face the others, she caught Mr McDonald's eyes on them, his brow slightly furrowed. She felt a pang of guilt at involving Miss Chiverton in something that had become perilous and resolved to alert the young lady to the threat.

Ewan's staff had arrived here before them and placed a tablecloth on a shaded piece of grass, on which now sat china plates, silver cutlery, goblets and a wide variety of food and drinks. There were even cushions provided for them all to sit on and, when they had made themselves comfortable and the ladies had arranged the long layers of their skirts around them, a footman handed them drinks and plates of food.

Mr Chiverton and Mr McDonald regaled the group with tales of Ewan's childhood exploits, which Lady Picton soon added her own recollections of, and a relaxed atmosphere fell over them. After the meal had been enjoyed in a leisurely manner, several people remained seated while the rest got up to explore the picturesque surroundings.

Miss Chiverton gave her a significant look, eyebrows raised, as she stood up and Ishbel nodded and strolled away in her company, leaving Ewan talking with his sister.

"Had you met Lady Tain?" Miss Chiverton asked, when she had recounted the events of the ball she had attended.

"No," Ishbel said as they walked through a small copse of trees, "and I feel it is no loss after what you have said of her."

"She was certainly unfeeling over Morag Duncan's death."

"I fear that there are many high-class people who would view the death of a working-class woman with a similar lack of concern. I am often shocked over the ability of my own class to treat those of lower social ranks as unimportant."

"Was Mr MacPherson injured because of your enquiries?"

Ewan had dismissed the questions about his injured arm, saying only that he had had an unfortunate misunderstanding with someone. Ishbel was not surprised that Miss Chiverton had guessed the truth.

"He was and, for that reason, I hope you will be reticent in your questions on our behalf in the future," she said. "I am grateful for your interest but the bullies who harmed Ewan made a threat to our lives, so they must not suspect you of being involved in the enquiry in any way."

"You will not give up the matter?" Miss Chiverton's response echoed their own anger at the violent attempt at controlling them.

"No, we shall not," Ishbel said firmly.

"Good. Now, I should not keep you from becoming better acquainted with Lady Picton, so that you may set a date for your wedding to Mr MacPherson."

Ishbel immediately smiled at this thought, imagining the event. A touch of superstition that she usually scorned had stopped her picturing the wedding as well as the life alongside Ewan that would follow it, but she longed for it to happen. Remembering something Ewan had told her, she said, "I must thank you for speaking on my behalf to Lady Picton. Ewan – Mr McPherson told me about it. That was good of you and I very much appreciate it."

"She cannot help but be glad you are marrying her brother when she knows you better," Miss Chiverton said earnestly.

Ishbel had misgivings on the likelihood of this but hoped wholeheartedly that she was right. They parted company and she looked in vain for Lady Picton and Ewan, walking in a circle that eventually led her back to the cluster of trees.

Miss Chiverton was still here and was speaking to Mr McDonald, saying forcefully, "I know that you are a good friend to Eddie but that gives you no leave to comment on my behaviour."

Ishbel hesitated, thinking she should leave them alone but suspecting that the conversation concerned what Miss Chiverton had done to help with the case, in which case she wished to speak in the young woman's defence.

"As a family friend," Mr McDonald was saying, "I am simply concerned that your youthful naiveté does not prevent you from seeing the risks..."

Miss Chiverton was positively seething with anger as she interrupted him. "... If you have any wish at all to be considered my friend, you will never again try to tell me what I can and cannot do!"

She stalked off and Ishbel hastily moved away, since Miss Chiverton certainly did not need anyone speaking up for her and she did not want to cause Mr McDonald any embarrassment if he realised she had overheard the argument. She could understand that he wished to help the young sister of his friend, if that was his only interest in Miss Chiverton, but his officious comments were certainly not endearing him to the lady.

She walked out of the trees and down the grassy slope to the loch, where she met Mr Chiverton, who was watching a couple of swans glide along the surface of the water, which reflected the green of the plants around it. He offered her his arm with a charming smile, oblivious to the disharmony between his sister and friend. She took it and they strolled along beside the loch. She wondered if she should mention the disagreement, but decided not to, since it had been a private quarrel that would hopefully soon be forgotten.

"My sister seems to have become your apprentice in the solving of crimes," he said with an amused look.

His calmness surprised her. "You do not object?"

"There would be little point. Fiona and I are alike in many ways, one being that when we make up our minds to do a thing, nothing and no one will dissuade us. Besides, I doubt anyone will be turning to her to catch murderers, so I do not have any reason for alarm just yet."

His attitude was a refreshing one and she relaxed and soon found herself laughing at another playful anecdote about Ewan. She looked up and caught a glimpse of Lady Picton's distinctive russet-coloured dress higher up on the grassy incline. She lifted her hand to wave, hoping they might be able to speak less formally without the rest of their party about, but the woman was already walking away, back towards the picnic food.

"Shall we rejoin them?" Mr Chiverton suggested, following her gaze.

"I would like that." They began to ascend the steep slope, arriving back at the refreshments area out of breath. Between the sun and the exertion Ishbel feared her face had been turned an unflattering shade of red, but there was nothing she could do so she put the thought out of her mind.

The rest of the group had already reassembled there and were sitting on cushions in the shade, being served food and drink by the footmen. Lord and Lady Picton were involved in a conversation with their children, while Miss Chiverton spoke to her brother. Ewan got to his feet and handed Ishbel and Mr Chiverton glasses of lemonade. "I fear I have no whisky to offer instead," he said to Mr Chiverton, who grinned.

"How remiss of you."

They were all smiling as they sat down on the cushions once more, Ishbel glad to rest since the unexpected heat had an enervating effect. The children darted off again, followed by their governess and there was a brief silence.

"You have brought the good weather with you from England," Ishbel said to Lord and Lady Picton, hoping that, in such lovely, relaxed surroundings, this would be a good time for them to all learn more about each other. She finished her drink, which was warm from the sun but still refreshing, and then handed the empty glass back to a footman, where she could do no damage with it. "We have not had the good fortune to enjoy so much sunshine since last summer."

"Perhaps your activities are more suited to the shadows," Lady Picton said.

The rest of the group reacted to this with startled expressions and Ishbel breathed in sharply as the words pierced her with their cold tone and implication of misconduct. She had no idea what had caused this new hostility and had no idea how to deal with it.

It felt as if Lady Picton had made up her mind to oppose the match between she and Ewan and she could only wonder miserably what she had done wrong this time.

41. A REQUEST FOR UNDERSTANDING

"DO YOU care nothing for my happiness?" Ewan demanded, when they got back to the house Lord Picton had rented for his family. The baron had left Ewan alone with his sister to conduct their conversation in private. "Why must you constantly treat Ishbel so unfairly?"

"I have given her every opportunity to show me a more ladylike side to her character and she has failed each time." Matilda did not raise her voice but her displeasure could not be mistaken as she stood by the unlit fireplace in the drawing room. The light from the candelabra was dim and left half her features in shadow, making it difficult to discern her expression. Not for the first time, Ewan had the sensation of speaking to someone he no longer understood, as she continued, "I do not know how you could possibly let yourself be so thoroughly deceived by Miss Campbell."

"In what way?" he asked, bewildered by her attitude. He could only assume this was about his wounded arm as there was nothing else he could think of that would have provoked this reaction. "I know you are worried that I was hurt, but you cannot possibly blame Miss Campbell for that. It is my decision to continue pursuing the exploration into Morag Duncan's death."

"I cannot influence you on that, but were you truly oblivious to Miss Campbell's shameless flirtation with Mr Chiverton at the picnic?"

Ewan could not stop the laugh of disbelief that burst out of him at this. "You could not have made a more absurd accusation."

"I saw them walking together un-chaperoned, arm-in-arm, speaking and laughing in the most intimate way."

This, at least, was a mistaken conclusion he could resolve and hopefully it would be the last of the problems between his sister and Ishbel. He walked over to her. "Matilda, in all the years you knew Chiverton before you left Scotland, did you ever see him pay the slightest attention to a woman?"

Her brow furrowed. "He was a young man with other interests."

"He was indeed. Since you will not let the matter rest without hearing the truth, I must speak it in the plainest way. Chiverton's affections are entirely bestowed on men rather than women."

Matilda gasped as she took in this revelation. "How could you speak so easily on such a subject? How can you remain friends with him?"

"I have known him for the majority of my life and, in the same way as he has not faltered in his friendship over my unconventional decisions, I have never for an instant wished to back away from my acquaintanceship with him. The subject is a private one that I must ask you never to repeat, even to your husband."

"I would not dream of it," she said, folding her arms, "or he would never allow you to be part of our lives. Ewan, you have never been led astray in such a manner?"

"My romantic feelings are entirely confined to women, specifically to Ishbel. I did not tell you this to lessen your opinion of Chiverton, whose friendship I will always value, but to show you how utterly wrong you were in what you thought you saw at the picnic."

"But Miss Campbell cannot know of Mr Chiverton's nature?"

"She does and, like me, she considers him a friend, one whom she may be at ease with in a way that an unmarried woman seldom can with a bachelor."

She shook her head, turning slightly away from him. "I thought, when we moved back to Edinburgh, that I would be returning to a brother I knew. I would never have believed that you could make the choices that you have." She sounded lost and sad.

"I was a child when you left and you were a naive woman, new to the ways of society and only just married. Is there nothing that you experienced without me where your life led you to events and decisions that you never imagined? Is there nothing that would surprise or even shock me?"

She stood lost in thought for a long moment before saying, "You are right. There were times when I acted in a way that I would have said as a child was impossible. I have not always been proud of myself and the events that gave me the most pleasure were not always what I would have expected."

He hoped that this admission would change her treatment of Miss Campbell, particularly now that she was aware of her wrong accusation. He walked up to her and put a hand on her shoulder. "You are my sister and I have missed out on too much of your life. Can we not allow each other to be changed by the years apart and accept those alterations like the loving siblings we once were?"

There were tears in her eyes as she said with feeling, "I would very much like to try."

They embraced and, as he held her gently, it felt for the first time as if he had got his sister back.

42. GOOD ADVICE

"HAS ANYONE of your acquaintance or anyone you have heard of been robbed in the last few months?" Ishbel asked Harriette after they broke their fast together and Lord Huntly left them to go to teach at the university.

"I have heard of two burglaries," Harriette replied as she sat working on a piece of embroidery in the drawing room. "Does this question have something to do with your latest corpse?"

"It does. Do either of the people or families robbed have a man with a temper who might seek revenge against the person responsible?"

"Your crime work does not seem to have made you particularly observant. It is not the master but the mistress of a home who would be more likely to be furious over being robbed. Her house is where she shows the world her accomplishments."

Ishbel had not considered this but it was just as possible that a woman had hired someone to kill Morag and to threaten her and Ewan. "Is that how you feel?" she asked curiously.

"Yes, it is," Harriette said, pulling her needle in and out of the piece of cloth in a steady rhythm. "I like to run my household efficiently and for dinner parties or other events I hold here to be perfect. I long ago gave up any expectation that you or Albion would notice anything I achieve here, so I do it for my own sake."

Lord Huntly seldom seemed to raise his head from a book or newspaper while he was in the house and Ishbel knew herself to be equally oblivious to the efforts Harriette made. "I am sorry."

"For what? You have your interests and I have mine. I have no complaints – on the contrary, I enjoy my life. I shudder to think what state your home will be kept in when you are married, though."

The comment reminded Ishbel of her current personal problems. "I have tried repeatedly to win Lady Picton's approval and I fear I am simply not someone she can ever approve of for her brother. If Ewan marries me, it could cost him his relationships with his sister and her family."

Harriette paused in her work. "If?" she said sharply.

"I wonder if it would be better for him were I to end the engagement," Ishbel said, hating to even think of such a thing but knowing how difficult it was for Ewan to be at odds with the sister he loved. He should not be forced to choose between them, facing the fear of losing not just his sister, but also his nieces and nephew from his life. "There has not yet been a formal announcement, so no one would be blamed or thought less..."

"... You fool!" Harriette snapped, throwing her embroidery down on the coffee table beside her. "Did you not learn your lesson the last time you took it upon yourself to decide what was best for Mr MacPherson? Did he appreciate you ending your association with him a few months ago? No, of course he did not. Would you want him making a similar decision that affected you without giving you any choice over it?" Without pause, she answered her own question. "No, you would not."

Her cousin was right. She would have been furious if Ewan had treated her the way she had treated him and he had been so hurt the last time she had sent him away. It would be unforgiveable for her to take another choice out of his hands.

Harriette continued, "Mr MacPherson is no more stupid than the average man, so he is perfectly capable of deciding whether or not he wishes to wed you. Does he?"

Ishbel found herself smiling. "He does."

"Then leave it at that." Harriette took up her embroidery again.

After a time Ishbel suggested, "Perhaps Ewan will be happy to continue running his own household after we are married?"

Harriette rolled her eyes. "It would not even surprise me."

43. THE REASON FOR THE THREATS

"THE QUESTION is why were we attacked?" Ewan said as they sat on chairs in the garden of Ishbel's house. "What information did we get too close to?"

The bruise on his cheek was no longer swollen but had turned a disturbing purple and yellow colour that looked painful. It made Ishbel feel oddly protective of him, which she knew must be an unfeminine reaction, but she did not care. When they were married she would be able to comfort him when he was hurt or ill – the shocking idea of embracing him and running her fingers through his dark hair brought warmth to her cheeks. She concentrated on his question.

"It must have been our enquiries into Morag's criminal activities that made someone worried of discovery," she said, looking out over the garden which now had several clumps of spring flowers blooming.

"I am not so sure," he said and she turned to him. "We had not asked about Morag selling on stolen items for some weeks and we had only just found out minutes before the attack that she might have been involved in the actual robberies."

"Harriette knows of a couple of families that had their houses robbed in the last few months. If someone had something personal stolen and was so angry that he or she hired someone to kill Morag, that person could also have hired criminals to watch and threaten us."

"That makes sense," Ewan said, "but I am concerned about the timing. You will recall the Jed found out that someone wanted us threatened on the day of the attack. We had asked nothing about robberies for weeks, so what could we have done that would make someone suddenly so afraid that they would hire people to harm us?"

"I see what you mean." She leaned her elbow on the arm of the chair and rested her chin on her hand. "We must have said or done something recently that made the murderer think we were close to finding them and if it was not the robberies..." She thought about the path their enquiries had taken. "... I can only think that it was our questions about Morag's father, but that makes no sense."

"Unless he is not dead. Perhaps he changed his name."

"Or Mrs Duncan put a false name on the Birth Certificate," Ishbel said. "I suppose if he were respectably married and Morag found him... No, it still seems impossible to me that he would have killed her."

"What if he had married for money and feared his wife's family would stop supporting him if his connection to Morag were discovered?"

"That is possible." Ishbel felt as if there was still a gap in their knowledge, something important that they did not know. "We wanted to protect Mrs Duncan from her husband finding out about her past, but she is the only one who can tell us who this man is."

Ewan stood up. "Then we must ask her."

44. AN UNEXPECTED SOLUTION

FIONA ARRIVED at his home, having escaped their parents' watchful eyes, while McDonald was already there, which neither party seemed happy about. Chiverton had noticed that something was amiss between them at the picnic, although neither had mentioned it, and he determined to get one or the other of them alone at some point today and learn what had happened. They were usually friends. Or they used to be. Actually, now he considered it, Fiona had not seemed in good humour towards McDonald for some time.

Alex winked at him and engaged Fiona in a conversation about the theatre, leaving Chiverton and McDonald free to continue their interrupted talk.

"I am sure Miss Campbell and MacPherson would be glad of any engagement gift," he said, wondering what he had missed, "although they would probably most appreciate it if you could tell them the identity of Robert McLennan."

"Who?"

"The father of the dead woman. MacPherson was telling me about their progress into the murder at the picnic."

"Why do you all pander to this morbid interest in dead people?" McDonald threw Fiona a dark look, which she did not seem to notice. "The sooner this enquiry is over, the better it will be for everyone."

"With the exception of Morag Duncan," Chiverton could not resist saying.

"Who?"

"The dead woman."

McDonald made a sour face.

"Miss Chiverton, is something wrong?" That was Alex's voice

and, hearing the words, Chiverton looked round.

Fiona was standing unmoving, with her eyes fixed on the window, a hand over her mouth. He walked over to her, McDonald at his heels.

"Fiona, what is it?" Chiverton asked, putting a hand on her shoulder. When she did not respond in any way he grew worried. "Fiona?"

"Miss Chiverton," McDonald said in the loud, slow way one might speak to a dense child, "what is wrong?"

This seemed to break through whatever had been controlling her thoughts and she looked round at them, wide-eyed. "I must go and find Miss Campbell without delay."

"Why?" Chiverton asked, confused.

"I believe I have worked out who committed the murder."

45. CLOSE TO THE TRUTH

"HOW COULD you possibly know about that?" Mrs Duncan turned so pale that Ewan feared she might faint when she realised that they knew she had not been married to Morag's father. "I am so ashamed."

"There is no need to be," Ishbel said and put a hand on Mrs Duncan's arm. "It is not for us to make any judgement, but we truly believe that Morag's father might have been responsible for her death. Could she have found him?"

Mrs Duncan lifted her gaze from her clasped hands, her eyes fearful at first but the expression fading when it became clear neither of them were looking at her with condemnation. "No, Robert could never injure Morag, let alone kill her. It's unthinkable."

"Robert McLennan was his real name?" Ewan asked. "Does he go by an alias now?"

"No. Not in the way you think. I want you to understand about him and me. He was a fun, handsome lad and when he began courting me I believed we would marry or I wouldn't have got as close to him as I did. But he was ambitious and I got impatient because he was studying all the time. We began to argue and we parted ways before I discovered I was going to have Morag. I thought of marrying him – I know he would have done it – but I was certain by then that we'd make each other unhappy. I couldn't have been the wife he needed and he wouldna have suited me. I had some money saved from working while I lived with my parents for many years, so I moved to a new part of the city where no one knew me and made up the tale of having a husband who died. A year later I met Mr Duncan."

"So McLennan never knew about his daughter?" Ishbel asked.

"Not for a long time. I... I saw him later and told him the truth because I needed him to help us, which he did."

"This was just before Morag's death?" Ewan guessed.

"No, it was years ago. He was still a good man and wanted to give me money to make our lives easier, but of course I couldna take it or Mr Duncan would learn the truth."

Ewan assumed that Mrs Duncan was either trying to fool herself or them, that the attempt to pay her had been a bribe to ensure the man never again had to see the woman he had left and the child he had never known. "But Morag did find out about her father before she died?"

"I'm not sure." Mrs Duncan looked sightlessly at the fire. "She would never leave the subject alone. Every few months she would ask me to tell her about her father and did he have any family she could meet and did he have a grave she could visit. So many questions and she just wouldna give up. So I told her that I hadna been married... The look she gave me, a mixture of disgust and horror; I'll never forget it. She left after that and she was dead a few days later."

"You told her the name of her father?" Ewan asked again.

"No. I dinna say anything about that. It's possible she could have worked out who he is but you couldna be more wrong if you think he would kill her. He's a decent man."

"Who is he, Mrs Duncan?" Ishbel said.

"I canna say. I can see that you dinna believe me about him and it would be too cruel for you to accuse him of such a thing. No." She shook her head. "That's the one thing I won't tell you."

She remained adamant on this issue, despite their entreaties, for some reason feeling she owed some loyalty to this man. At last they were forced to give up and they left her, so close to knowing all, but with the last crucial piece of knowledge missing.

46. A CHANGE OF HEART

"A FEW people have called on you in your absence, miss, including Lady Picton," the butler said as he took Ewan and Ishbel's outdoor clothing from them, "and Her Ladyship is entertaining them in the drawing room."

Ishbel shot Ewan an appalled look, which he returned and they hastened to the room. Ishbel took a deep breath before opening the door and she and Ewan found themselves looking upon not just Harriette and Lady Picton, but also Miss Chiverton, Mr Chiverton and Mr McDonald.

Lady Picton got to her feet but, before Ishbel could beg her not to leave, certain Harriette must have offended her, Ewan's sister said, "I appear to have called at an inopportune moment but might I speak to you for a few minutes alone, Miss Campbell?" She smiled at both Ishbel and Ewan as she spoke, which reassured Ishbel that unaccountably all was well.

"Yes, of course."

Leaving Ewan with the rest of the guests, whose combined presence here she could not fathom, Ishbel led Lady Picton into the dining room. They took seats at right angles to each other at the dining table.

"May I send for refreshments for you?" Ishbel asked.

"I have already enjoyed two cups of chocolate," Lady Picton said, with an amused smile.

"I am so sorry I was not here when you arrived."

"It is not important." Lady Picton cleared her throat. "I was rude to you at the picnic."

"I did not know why you were angry."

"Ewan did not tell you about my misconception?"

"No."

"Oh, dear." Lady Picton put a hand to her cheek and then lowered it again. "I saw you walking alone with Mr Chiverton, speaking in an intimate manner, and I thought..." She broke off, but Ishbel could see quite clearly what she had imagined and could not help but smile. "... Yes, I can see that you are entirely aware of why Mr Chiverton would never behave romantically towards you."

Ishbel said, "Mr Chiverton is a good man and a friend to both Ewan and me."

"I must confess that I am astonished that either of you would wish to continue your acquaintanceship with him after you discovered the truth, but that is your decision."

"I was surprised – even rather shocked – when Ewan told me the truth about Mr Chiverton's nature. It is unusual but I have come to feel that his search for happiness is no stranger than my own. He and I are both, in different ways, misfits who can never be entirely ourselves in high society."

"But what he does is immoral," Lady Picton said, brow furrowed.

"He wants to be loved. Would it be better for him to pretend an affection he could never feel for a woman and convince her falsely to marry him?"

"No," Lady Picton said. "Perhaps not."

"Mr Chiverton has been extremely kind to me and has always taken Ewan's side, even when he was not easy about the criminal enquiries."

"You have given me something to consider, but that is not the subject I came here to speak about. I was wrong when I judged you to be an unsuitable lady for Ewan. I may never understand the interest in crime the two of you have, but my brother loves you and I have come to respect your intelligence and the kindness you show to people around you."

"Then we have your blessing to be married?" Ishbel asked hopefully.

"You do."

This unexpected change of attitude made Ishbel's emotions swell and, to her embarrassment, she felt tears running down her cheeks. "Excuse me." She wiped them away but they kept flowing. "I am so glad..."

Lady Picton leaned over to put an arm round her shoulders and they exchanged a brief hug. "We are family now. Everything will be well."

And Ishbel finally believed it.

47. WHAT MISS CHIVERTON KNOWS

EWAN WAS eager to share Miss Chiverton's deductions with Ishbel, but he paused at the sight of her walking into the room with Matilda at her side, both of them smiling.

He walked over to them and Matilda said, "You must tell me as soon as the two of you set a date for the wedding. My whole family will look forward to attending."

Ewan was not sure how she intended to win over her husband, but he was overwhelmed with pleasure at her words. After their last conversation he had hoped she would want to resolve matters with Ishbel. He took his sister's hand and smiled at both women, who looked equally happy now that their differences were finally settled and they could start to become friends.

"Have you told Miss Campbell who the murderer is?" Miss Chiverton asked excitedly, approaching the three of them.

"You know who he is?" Ishbel exclaimed, looking at Miss Chiverton.

Ewan thought ruefully that it would have been pleasant to have a moment alone with Ishbel to set a date for their wedding, but apparently that would have to wait. He turned to his sister. "You will not wish to hear about this."

"In fact, I am a little curious," Matilda confessed.

"I heard the name Robert mentioned at the ball," Miss Chiverton was saying to Ishbel, "and as soon as Eddie said that Morag's father was called Robert McLennan, I knew it was he, because of the association between them."

"I do not follow," Chiverton said as he and McDonald joined their circle by the drawing room door.

"Nor do I," Ishbel agreed. "Who is the man?"

"Ishbel," Lady Huntly interrupted, "at least allow your guests to be seated. You are responsible for their comfort now." Her tone implied that she had done more than enough entertaining of people she barely knew in Ishbel's absence.

"Yes, of course," she said. "Thank you."

Lady Huntly left them to continue their discussion without her and Ishbel encouraged the preoccupied group to sit down. Ewan caught Matilda's bemused expression as she joined them.

"It is Lord Tain," Miss Chiverton said.

"Of course! That makes sense of everything." Ishbel looked towards Ewan, more quickly understanding the situation than he had. "He became a lord through his legal work, so his name changed. No one would think of him as Robert McLennan anymore."

He added, "Mrs Duncan said Morag's father had helped them and she must have been talking about the theft when Morag was twelve." This had to be explained to the rest of the group, who listened with varying expressions and levels of interest, Miss Chiverton the most curious to understand everything and McDonald, the least.

"Mrs Duncan must have told Lord Tain he was Morag's father to encourage him to assist her," Ishbel said, eyes bright, "which he did when he ensured she would not be punished for the theft."

"He must have thought the situation could remain private at the time, with Mrs Duncan so keen to keep the truth from her husband, but Morag realised years later that he was her father and went to see him at the law courts," he said.

"It would destroy his legal career and reputation were it to be known that he had an illegitimate daughter," Miss Chiverton joined in. "That was how I knew he had a strong reason for the murder."

"He has a cruel side to his personality that I never guessed at," Ishbel said, remembering the apparent concern Lord Tain had shown over Morag's death. His real fear must have been that he would be found out and, of course, having been alerted by them to their enquiry into the death, he probably had them watched from that point on. She shivered to think of someone following them for so long, ready to harm or perhaps even kill them if they got close to finding out the truth.

"He would have known plenty of criminals from his work that he could hire to attack us," Ewan said, his thoughts moving in the same direction as hers.

Ishbel turned to Miss Chiverton with a smile. "You have found the explanation to the murder. This explains every detail."

"Now," Ewan said, "we just have to arrest him."

48. MAKING AN ARREST

THEY FOUND two members of the Town Guards to accompany them to Lord Tain's home, getting the address from Jed Cassell. It was mid-evening by the time they arrived, late enough that he should be at home. The street was high up, looking over much of the city, and the house was in a secluded patch of countryside.

"So this is what a man will kill his own child to keep," Ishbel said, looking up at the building. It resembled a small castle in size and because of its rounded turrets and medieval appearance. She imagined Lord Tain growing up poor but dreaming of becoming wealthy and powerful and, unlike many, he had put in the considerable amount of work necessary to turn a thought into reality. As a solicitor, he must have once cared about justice – how could he have lost his humanity to such a degree?

Ewan used the door knocker and a smartly dressed butler answered and invited them inside.

"We'll wait here," one of the guards said and the men hung back in the large hall.

She and Ewan were shown into a drawing room twice the size of her family's where Lord and Lady Tain were sitting with three young children. Ishbel's heart lurched at the sight of the innocent young faces – she had not considered that he might have children. It was like spotting a wolf amid a flock of lambs.

"Miss Campbell and Mr MacPherson, is that right?" Lord Tain said, his expression genial. "Are you here in connection with Morag Duncan?"

"We are, sir," Ewan answered.

Lord Tain introduced his wife to them. She was younger than he by some years and had an attractive face that was marred by the haughtiness of her expression. She had a maid take the children away but made it clear that she hoped this visit would be a brief one. Ishbel supposed this was not surprising if she feared their evening being disrupted by a legal matter. It was Lord Tain's attitude that was disconcerting to Ishbel – he seemed to have no fear of what their presence here meant.

They refused refreshments and, when they had all sat down, Lord Tain said, "Have you found any more about what happened to Morag Duncan?"

"We know everything," Ishbel said and received only a raised eyebrow in reaction. "Morag was your daughter." He started at this, his smile vanishing. "You only found out about her when she was twelve and came to see you with her parents. Her mother begged for your help, which you gave. You presumably imagined that you would never see Morag again, but she came to see you on the day she died."

"A week before then actually," Lord Tain said, surprising her with his willingness to discuss Morag. "She wasna sure if she was right about who I was and I confirmed I was her father. She had not had an easy life and there were things troubling her she would not tell me about, but it was a fond reunion nonetheless."

"You claim you were happy that she found out you were her father?" Ewan said, exchanging a confused glance with Ishbel.

"Of course I was," he said, with such a strong appearance of honesty that Ishbel began to wonder if they had solved the murder or been entirely wrong in the conclusions that had led them here. "We arranged to meet on the day of her death for a longer conversation as we both still had a great many questions for each other. I confessed everything to my wife." He looked over at Lady Tain and Ishbel took in the lady's pallor and pinched lips.

The puzzle pieces rearranged themselves and Ishbel said, "You told Lady Tain when you would see Morag next?"

Ewan shot her a perplexed look at this change in direction.

"Yes, of course," Lord Tain said. "I wanted Morag to be a part of our lives."

Ishbel heard Ewan's intake of breath as he reached the same conclusion as her.

"Did you ever see Morag again?" she asked.

"Yes, she arrived as arranged and we talked for about an hour. I had to defend a client in court, but I gave Morag a little money and she agreed to let me find her a small house to live in. It should have been the start of our relationship and instead it was the end. It's haunted me that the money I gave her might have been the cause of her murder – that some thief wanted to steal it and killed her to get it. Is that what you think happened?"

He looked trustingly at them and, with all their notions altered, Ishbel's heart ached for him. Her judgement of his character when she met him had been right after all: he truly was the good man he had always appeared to be.

"No," she said quietly. "A thief did not kill her, did they, Lady Tain?"

Lord Tain followed Ishbel's gaze to his wife. "Sophia?" he said.

Lady Tain's mouth flattened into a thin line as she looked back at him. "I will not discuss this in front of strangers."

"Aye, you will," Lord Tain said firmly.

She looked as if she would refuse to respond, but finally she seemed to make up her mind, addressing her words to her husband. "She was a common little wretch who strode into your life and, instantly, you would have let her destroy the life we had created." Her voice shook with emotion. "Did you think no one else would find out about her? You would not listen to my fears and so I had to protect my family from that woman."

"What did you do?" Lord Tain was looking at his wife as if he did not know her.

"I took a knife with me and waited while you and the girl talked. When she left I followed her. The route she took around the back of the law courts was perfect – there was no one else in the alley and it meant I could wipe my hands clean and return to my coach with no one seeing a thing. There were spots of blood down the front of my dress but I made up an excuse to the servants about a fight breaking out between two criminals. That should have ended it, but then the two of you began asking questions," she said, looking coldly at Ishbel and Ewan, "and I realised at a ball recently, when someone else mentioned it, that you would not give up. I had one of my footmen hire men to scare you off, hurt you if they had to, but you would not listen. What will it take? Money?"

"Do you actually think you will not have to pay for such an evil crime?" Lord Tain asked her and the look she gave him said just that.

"I did it for our family," she said to him, as if that excuse would make everything all right.

"Morag was my daughter," he said in an anguished tone. "Our family could have survived anything except this."

Ewan got up and brought the two guards into the room. Lady Tain looked from them to her husband as if she could not believe what was happening. "Robert, stop this. It is your duty to help me."

"You have committed murder, Sophia. No one can help you."

Lady Tain was still protesting as she was taken away by the guards, clearly horrified that she would be held accountable for the murder.

When she and the guards were gone, silence descended.

"I am so sorry that you have to suffer this," Ishbel said to Lord Tain, who was like a faded shadow of the man he had been just minutes ago.

"I never understood her at all," he said, more to himself than them. "I never imagined she could harm anyone, let alone..." He broke off.

Ewan patted his shoulder. "You still have your children to be of comfort to you."

"Not all of them," Lord Tain said.

EPILOGUE

Five Months Later

"NO MATTER what one might say about her character, Miss Campbell does make a lovely bride," Lady Selman conceded as she and her husband sat and watched the lady in question walk beside Lord Huntly to the front of the church to join Mr MacPherson and the vicar.

"One wonders why they were in such haste to wed," her husband said.

"Indeed! And now they have had another member of the peerage arrested and, after we have suffered the indignity of seeing one of our own in court, Lady Tain is to be hanged. Their actions are unpardonable."

"But slightly less so than Lady Tain's," her husband commented, which she felt was beside the point.

"One does not expect the people one meets in society to run about chasing murderers."

"Quite."

"Lady Huntly must be delighted to finally get Miss Campbell off her hands, when the lady looked sure to stay a spinster for life." She craned her head to see Lady Huntly, who was wearing a breathtaking blue gown and seemed to be wiping her eyes. "It astonishes me that Mr MacPherson did not choose better for himself, though: such a woman! Such a blemished reputation!" She nudged her husband, who had been looking with a smile at Miss Campbell, who did look uncommonly beautiful in a gown that had flowers embroidered across it. Lady Selman did not normally find red-hair flattering but there was no doubt that both Miss Campbell and Lady Huntly came from a handsome family. Mr MacPherson was – had been until now – one of Edinburgh's most attractive bachelors, so the pair would undoubtedly have striking offspring. Perhaps that was the appeal of the match to him, as Miss Campbell was known to have little inheritance.

The vicar asked the usual questions and it seemed as if everyone in the church held their breaths in anticipation when he came to the line, "If anyone has reason why these two should not be joined in matrimony may they speak now or forever hold their peace."

Would Lady Picton object? Would Mr MacPherson change his mind? Lady Selman strained forward, trying to look in every direction at once, but alas, there was no objection to enliven the day.

The ceremony came to an end and Lady Selman gasped as Mr MacPherson and his new bride kissed each other in public with a most indecent display of passion. Miss Campbell – Mrs MacPherson now – should have been told that one did not show such affection for one's own husband.

Lady Selman got to her feet as the married couple passed by, not wanting to be the last out of the church. She put a hand over her eyes as she stepped out into the sunshine, Lord Selman at her side, and saw Mr and Mrs MacPherson exchange embraces and comments with their friends and family, of whom there were surprisingly many.

The couple waved as they got into an open-topped carriage and then they were leaving, off on an exciting journey, no doubt. Not that Lady Selman in any way envied them for having such adventurous lives.

The crowd began to disperse, although she noticed that Lady Huntly and Lady Picton stood arm-in-arm watching until the carriage was out of sight. Who would have expected two such different ladies to find common ground?

"I suppose we shall have to find something else to do now," Lord Selman remarked with a frown. "How tedious."

Thanks for reading

Thank you so much for taking an interest in my books. If you enjoyed this novel please would you consider leaving a review at Amazon or Goodreads as this is a massive help to independent authors in getting our books known. It also helps other readers learn more about the books, so they can decide whether to buy them.

Join the Fun

My website is https://clarejayne.com and includes a blog about books and historical facts. You can also join my e-mail newsletter there and get a free eBook novella, "**Harriette**", which tells of the events which turn a naive young woman into the fierce Lady Huntly from the *Campbell & MacPherson* novels. You will also get a sequel to "**Complications**", a guide to the historical world and characters from the *Campbell & MacPherson* series and the latest information about my new novels and special offers.

OTHER NOVELS AVAILABLE AT AMAZON

"Lady Tinbough's Dilemma (Campbell & MacPherson 1)" - Ishbel is interested in only her studies. Ewan is interested in only Ishbel. They make the unlikeliest detectives imaginable.

Ishbel Campbell lives in Georgian era Edinburgh and hates the uselessness of high society life with its constant balls and dinner parties, escaping it by the shocking means of attending lectures at the city's university. She decided long ago that she would never marry. With the wealth of a large estate to give him a life of luxury, Ewan MacPherson loves this world and believes the only thing missing from it is a wife.

Ishbel and Ewan meet at the trial of masked gentleman thief, William Brodie. This interest in crime leads to them being given the task of finding a missing emerald necklace. Ishbel only agrees to appease her cousin and Ewan only does so to spend more time with Ishbel. With no idea of what they are doing, they are close to giving up when they discover that a young maid has disappeared. In a time before the police force ever existed, no one but them cares about the fate of a working-class woman, so they are determined to find her.

As the danger rises and jealousies and insecurities threaten their partnership, will they be able to solve the mystery in time or will the criminal's deadly attentions turn on them?

"The Dead Duke (Campbell & MacPherson 2)" - When Ishbel and Ewan take on the case of a duke supposedly murdered by his actress mistress, Lady Huntly threatens to disown Ishbel while Edinburgh's upper classes are appalled, and that is before the duo even begin looking into the reasons why the wealthiest members of society might have wanted the duke dead.

As they continue to uncover secrets others want to remain hidden, their own relationship is threatened by the public discovery of a scandal from Ishbel's past. Is her repeated refusal to follow society's conventions about to ruin her life as well as her partnership with Ewan, and will they ever manage to solve the mystery of who murdered the duke?

"The Convenient Murder (Campbell & MacPherson 4)" - The unconventional Georgian-era detectives, Ishbel and Ewan, have a new murder to investigate when Lord Strand is poisoned at a house where their friends, Miss Chiverton and McDonald, are staying.

Miss Chiverton seems determined that the murder be solved, so why is she hiding important information about it? Lord Strand's relatives all appear more relieved than grief-stricken over the death and everyone who ever met the man seems to have hated him, so the list of suspects is endless.

In the meantime, Miss Chiverton's father is determined that she should make a decision about who to marry or he will choose for her. The man who is desperately in love with her is the last person she wants and all she can focus on is helping to solve the murder.

As events grow more hazardous, lives change and not everyone will emerge unscathed.

"Mr Guthrie's Double (Campbell & MacPherson 5)" - A killer is about to strike but which Mr Guthrie is he after?

Ishbel and Ewan, are given a bizarre new case when they have to hunt down an imposter who has been falsely claiming to be Mr Guthrie.

The real Mr Guthrie is a likeable man from a wealthy family who wins the affection of Miss Chiverton. This complicates everyone's lives as Ewan's friend, Mr McDonald, also loves her and her family only approves of Mr McDonald as a suitor, so Miss Chiverton will face a difficult decision about her future.

The case soon grows more strange and more deadly when a corpse is found, but it won't be the last death as Ishbel and Ewan desperately work to uncover the reason for the impersonator's deception.

"A Virtuous Man (Campbell & MacPherson 6)" - Why would a seemingly honourable university student vanish one night and never return home?

After Ishbel and Ewan leave Edinburgh, the newly married Mr and Mrs McDonald inherit their missing person case, much to Padraig's annoyance. He is sure the young man must have gone off alone to have fun and Padraig would rather concentrate on life with his new bride than deal with it. The missing man is a devout

Catholic, though, so it seems increasingly unlikely that he ran off in this way. They then discover that a second man went missing on the same night as the first.

As the missing person case grows more baffling, it causes arguments between Fiona and Padraig - whose marriage might not be as stable as they thought - and the longer the matter remains unsolved, the more likely it is that the boy will die before they can find him.

"An Impossible Crime (Campbell & MacPherson 7)" - Things are not going well for Ishbel and Ewan. Ishbel is miserable living in the countryside, Ewan hates how much time she spends with the local physician and they have a new murder to solve.

Ishbel was looking forward to returning to Edinburgh soon, but now that plan has had to be changed. She is bored and frustrated living on the country estate where Ewan grew up, while he has plenty to do and spends little time at home. She only has two real friends nearby – James Fraser, a physician, and Emma Lee, a spinster.

It is James who tells them of Lady Ashton's death and of his professional belief that she was smothered with a pillow. Both Lady Ashton's husband and cousin had reasons to kill her, but unfortunately it seems impossible for them to have done so.

James takes an interest in their hunt for the killer, Ewan growing less civil every time he finds him at the house, and then Emma falls under suspicion for the crime. Tensions rise between Ishbel and Ewan to the point where their marriage is threatened and a final twist might have even more devastating consequences for them.

"The Prankster (Campbell & MacPherson 8)" - When is a joke not a joke?

Miss Emma Lee, neighbour to Ishbel and Ewan, is being disturbed by a series of bizarre pranks involving her late father's hat. Unnerved by it and bemused as to why she is the unknown culprit's target, she turns to the duo for help.

They are still living on their country estate, Ishbel having given birth to Meg, their second child, recently. Emma is one of Ishbel's closest friends and she and Ewan believe this will be a quick, safe mystery to solve, bringing no danger to their family. They are wrong on both accounts.

When the prankster's tricks turn deadly, no one is safe. The amateur detectives must use all their skills to protect their neighbours and their own lives whilst solving the riddle of who is responsible and why.

"Murder on Bealtaine Eve (Dumnonia Mysteries 1)" With blood spilt during a sacred ceremony, will the gods forgive her people?
In fifth century Dark Ages England, Morvoren is the priestess of Dumnonia, serving the goddess who protects them. She is confident of her place as one of the most important people in the tribe, with the respect of the king and love of her people. At least, that's what she thinks.

The inexplicable murder of a Saxon guest throws all her assumptions about her life into confusion and makes her fear retribution from her goddess. Forced to work with Uxio, a young Christian deacon who hates her religion, she must solve the crime or lose her home and her freedom.

Uxio is ordered to work with Morvoren by his bishop, but this tribe brings back far too many memories of a past he has tried to forget. Morvoren's uncanny ability to see more than he wants to reveal puts them at odds and a second murder adds to the tension between them. With the possibility of war between the Dumnonii and the Saxons looming over them, they struggle to hunt down an elusive killer.

This unique historical mystery series is set against the backdrop of Celtic beliefs and one tribe's struggle to survive in the changing land of Britannia.

"Fatal Voyage (Dumnonia Mysteries 2)" - Will Morvoren and Uxio discover a killer or a vengeful ghost?
With the approach of the Samhain festival to honour the dead, the captain of a merchant ship tells Morvoren an eerie tale of a voyage plagued by misfortune, illness and death, wanting her, as Dumnonia's priestess, to help rid him of its source. The captain is sure that the two deaths are from natural causes, since no one could have got to the second man, whose body was found blocking the door to his cabin. Despite this, the Christian deacon, Uxio believes the problems are the result of a murderer onboard.

Circumstances and their different personalities cause Uxio and Morvoren to quarrel yet again over how to find out the truth, so they make a wager to investigate the mystery separately. Each one will try to be the first to discover how two people on the ship died.

There seems to be no link between the dead men and no way for them to have been murdered, but both had their enemies. As Morvoren and Uxio struggle to make sense of the mystery, what fresh troubles will they face? They are both determined to best the other, but will a killer outwit them both?

This is the second novel in this exciting historical mystery series set in the Celtic Dumnonii tribe in England in the Dark Ages, a time of turmoil with conflicting beliefs and cultures.

"The Vanishing Thief (Dumnonia Mysteries 3)" - How could someone disappear from a castle on a cliff with stolen treasure, never being seen by the guards at its only entrance?

The latest mystery infuriates the king, confuses the warriors protecting the castle and needs to be solved by Morvoren and Uxio. While Morvoren deals with a problem with her closest friend and Uxio struggles to cope with a servant with a crush on him, they must somehow work out how the impossible theft was committed.

The subsequent appearance of a dead body doesn't help in the least.

"Murder By Another Name (Dumnonia Mysteries 4)" - When is a crime not a crime? Morvoren, the priestess of the Dumnonii in Dark Age Britain, has to travel most of the length to solve a new mystery that the chieftan, Comux, can't deal with. Kenosaglas has killed his life-long friend, Eudaf, claiming that Eudaf was a spy for the nearby Saxons. If Kenosaglas is telling the truth then he cannot be punished for his actions. If he killed Eudaf for another reason, Kenosaglas is a murderer who will probably face execution.

Morvoren faces a seemingly unsolvable puzzle since no one witnessed Eudaf's death except for his killer. Even the two men's families can tell her nothing helpful and Kenosaglas's own children insist that Eudaf was not a traitor. Her search for the truth leads her to another confrontation with the Saxon leader who once wanted to marry her.

In the meantime, the Christian deacon Uxio has been left behind at Bran Castle and has a reunion that leaves his future in question.

The danger increases for Morvoren, who is under the protection of Comux, the son of the queen who hates her. When her life depends on it, will she be able to trust him?

Read the fourth historical mystery novel in this exciting series set in a time where an argument can end in a sword fight and people believe in giants and pixies.

"**Ladies Dancing**" - Three people find romance over a magical winter season.

In Regency England Kate and Louisa arrive in London - accompanied by Kate's brother, Will - to make their debuts into London society and find themselves husbands. Kate encounters Mr Templeton, who is the opposite of everything she thinks she wants in a man. He might soon change her mind, though, if her blunt manners do not ruin everything.

Her cousin, Louisa, wants to get a wealthy husband as quickly as possible for her own secret reasons. Why she should soon decide to turn down a good-natured earl is a mystery and Kate is determined to find out what she is hiding. The truth might prove to be more than she can cope with.

There is also her brother, Will, to worry about. As a wealthy, attractive gentleman, he could easily find himself a wife... if only he did not loathe every person he encounters, with the notable exception of the charming Mr Fenton. To make the best of the situation, Kate intends to throw the two men at each other as much as possible to keep Will from scaring off their potential suitors. She never imagines the attachment that might form between Will and Mr Fenton.

Just as the duo are making progress in their romantic adventures, a scandal is revealed that threatens to devastate their lives.

If you enjoy the romance, family drama and humour of a Georgette Heyer story, you will love this festive historical novel.

"**Complications**" - This is a light-hearted Georgian era romance where, in the hunt for the right gentleman, nothing works out as intended.

Amelia Daventry dreams of having the lovely clothes and luxuries her family cannot afford. She intends to use her Edinburgh season to get herself the wealthiest and most powerful husband she can find. The one thing of which she is certain is that Mr Brightford, with his constant frowns and criticisms, is a man she would never consider.

Amelia's best friend, Lottie Harrington, has found the man she wants to marry and just wishes to live quietly and make him happy. Her hopes are about to be destroyed, causing pain and chaos to herself and everyone around her.

Lottie's headstrong brother, Benjamin Harrington, has romantic feelings for other men but his parents still expect him to marry. When he meets a man he can love he faces difficult choices but does the gentleman even return his affection?

From suffering heartbreak and tragedy to fighting a duel, the lives of these three friends are about to become extremely complicated…

"An Impetuous Romance" - Will Adam bring Eloise happiness or break her heart?

Miss Eloise Preston is thrilled when the kind, handsome Lord Adam Delworth arrives in Somerset and shows an interest in her, unaware that his offer of marriage has just been turned down by someone he believes to have been the love of his life. To get her out of a dangerous situation, he asks her to marry him and, believing that he loves her, she gladly agrees.

They go to London accompanied by her sisters, Maddie and Helena. Adam immediately encounters his first love again and he is torn between the two women. In the meantime, London society - with its own rules of conduct - is causing the sisters to make one blunder after another. To add to their problems, Helena Preston is thrown into the company of the man she rejected, whom her father is determined she should still marry.

The lives and loves of Eloise, Adam, Helena and Maddie are all connected in this heart-warming Regency romance. If you enjoy the humour, twists and turns, and gentle romance of a Georgette Heyer novel, this is the perfect book for you.

ABOUT THE AUTHOR

Clare Jayne began writing novels when she was a teenager. She has worked in a variety of jobs, including legal secretary and sales advisor, while continuing to write and she began self-publishing about ten years ago.

Inspired by such writers as Jane Austen, Josephine Tey and Georgette Heyer, she writes historical romances and historical mysteries, although the mysteries also have a strong dash of romance.

Clare lives in the Highlands of Scotland and counts the Loch Ness Monster as a close neighbour. She is an animal lover and vegetarian. When she is not writing or researching different time periods to write about, she can be found trying to read twenty different novels at the same time.

You can find out more about Clare Jayne at her website (clarejayne.com) or on Twitter or Goodreads.

Printed in Great Britain
by Amazon

62686167R00099